Tinker's Tim and the Witches

Tinker's Tim
and the Witches

by BERTHA C. ANDERSON

Illustrations by Lloyd Coe

LITTLE, BROWN AND COMPANY · *Boston*

Published simultaneously
in Canada by McClelland and Stewart Limited

PRINTED IN THE UNITED STATES OF AMERICA

This book is dedicated to the boys and girls I have known through the years, for they have filled me with a desire to write stories for young people; and to the memory of my mother, who believed in my writing.

Contents

Tinker's Tim and the Witches

1. Tim Finds Trouble

THE July sun was hot, and Tim was tired by the time he finished weeding the vegetable bed. He rubbed the sweat from his freckled face with the rough sleeve of his homespun jacket, shook back his tousled, copper-colored hair. Then he got to his feet, stretching the cramps from his legs.

All day he had heard the tap, tap of his father's mallet on wood, and wondered what he could be making. He had not dared ask, or go to the workshop to see.

Tim was proud of his father, for he could mend almost anything. Because they lacked a better name for such a clever workman, the people of Salem called him the Tinker. The boy had often watched him whittle out a cherrywood dasher for a churn, which turned out better than the housewife's first dasher had been. All over town he had put shutters and latches, spinning wheels and looms, furniture and kitchenware in fine order.

Tim thought about the tapping of the mallet. There was no work to be done for the townspeople, for when Tim had last gone with the Tinker to the houses along Town House Lane seeking work, doors had been slammed in their faces. The whole town was suddenly unfriendly to the Tetlows.

Tim looked at his hands, grubby from weed pulling. Granny expected him to be tidy. He sauntered down the path to the spring, the sound of the Tinker's mallet growing fainter to his ears.

Taking the gourd dipper from its peg on a nearby tree, he poured water slowly over one hand, then over the other, and watched the muddy water trickle away over the stones. Then, looking up, he caught a glimpse of someone moving among the trees. Sturdy John, the shipbuilder's son, followed by lanky Ethan, son of a millwright, stepped into the path some distance ahead.

A smile of relief spread over Tim's face. The last time he had gone to the wharves to play, John and Ethan had run from him. But here they were now, near his own home! "My weed pulling is done. Come spin the new top I made with one of Father's knives." Enticingly, he pulled the top from among the other treasures in his pocket and held it up.

John lifted his chin and thrust his hands into his pockets. "My father says I am not to play with you," he said shortly.

"Mine, too." Ethan pursed his lips primly, and moved a little closer to John.

Tim's face puckered with bewilderment. Seeing them here, Tim had begun to hope that the two boys would be friends with him again. "If you will not play, why are you here?" he challenged.

Ethan looked at John. It was John who spoke.

[5]

"We thought we might see the witch who lives hereabouts."

Tim's blue eyes stretched wide with fear. Tales of the evil work of witches, which the boys had whispered to him down by the wharves, had made the shivers creep down his spine. But now they were here, near his own door, looking for witches.

"There are no witches about!" Tim said, his voice sounding strange and muffled.

"So! Was not Dame Whitcomb bewitched until she died of it?" John asked with a scornful lift of his eyebrows.

Tim wanted to cry out in denial of this terrible thought, but the words stuck in his tight throat. He stood silently gripping the handle of the gourd dipper with one hand and his new top with the other, while the two boys went away down the path. Then he hung up the dipper and thrust the top deep into his pocket.

He scarcely knew how he reached the door of the Tinker's workshop. But, now that he was here, he knew that he could not tell his father of the words John had said. Granny had been with

[6]

Dame Whitcomb every day she was sick, and surely she would know that no witches were about!

Standing in the door, Tim watched his father bent over his work. He was a lean little man, with hair the color of Tim's though it was gone from the top of his head. Sweat ran down his face in dirty streaks. As he worked, he hummed a little tune under his breath.

By now Tim's curiosity about what his father was making was getting the best of him. "Nosey," Granny called him. "What are you afraid of?" he asked himself. John and Ethan were afraid of their stern and solemn fathers, but the Tinker was different.

Tim cleared his throat. "What are you making, Father?"

The Tinker straightened slowly. "A trap to catch meddlers," he said dryly.

Tim chuckled and let out his breath in a puff of relief. The old twinkle was in his father's eye. The fathers of John and Ethan would never think of jesting as his father did. And, as for singing, they would allow only psalms. His father sang such lilting tunes that Tim thought the birds sometimes stopped to listen. Looking about the shop, Tim noticed that a piece of sailcloth lay over something in a corner. He would give his new top for a good, honest peek under it.

Near his father lay a pile of straight, wooden pieces. His father was forming a stout circle of wood. Wheels, Tim thought, but what for?

Then he blurted out, "Why are you making wheels, Father?"

"Who said I was making wheels?" Tim's father turned and scowled at his son.

"Why-y, there are the spokes and rims," Tim stammered, pointing.

"It could still be only a contraption for catching meddlers." But the Tinker's next words were quite serious. "It would not be well to mention the making of wheels to Ethan and John, lad."

Tim curled his bare toes in the shavings and frowned at them. "As for Ethan and John — they are not my friends any more."

The Tinker looked at him keenly. "Did you vex

[8]

them, lad? If you did, you must ask forgiveness."

"No, Father, I did not. They run from me and will not play with me. I cannot learn the trouble." Tim bit his lip to keep it from trembling.

"How long?" the Tinker quizzed gently.

"For days and — days! I — I think, I must go now," Tim mumbled.

"Have you finished your tasks, Tim? Busy hands at useful work keep the heart from aching." His father cocked an eye at the afternoon sun. "The Sabbath will be here before we know it. It is time to bring Daisy to be milked, and the mare to be tethered close by. We must do nothing to bring down the anger of a tithing man on us — now."

"Yes, Father." And Tim was off to the village meadows.

He dreaded the Sabbath, for there were so many hard-to-remember laws to keep. There could be no play; no work done; no journey made. Older lawbreakers were fined, while for unruly children tithing men carried switches. They were spies — those tithing men, always about, especially at the beginning of the Sabbath. And it was the

longest day of the week, beginning with the laying aside of tasks and play at three o'clock on
Saturday, and ending at sundown on Sunday.

When Tim came to the pasture, he saw that
cows belonging to other townspeople were still
grazing. At some distance Tim could tell Daisy
from the other cows, though they were spotted
red and white, much the same as she. Most of the
others wore pieces of red cloth to keep them from
being bewitched. Daisy did not. Granny said it
was foolish.

Yet, Tim often felt afraid. There was that terrible day last week when Tim knew vaguely that
witches were being hanged on Gallows Hill. He
had heard the crowds go by, some distance from
their cottage. But he had been kept busy with tasks
all day. Now his meeting with John and Ethan
by the spring made him uneasy.

Daisy was lying in the shade of a big tree at the
edge of the meadow, contentedly chewing her
cud. She looked no more bewitched than the cows
flaunting red rags.

Tim pulled a switch from a tree and stripped it

of leaves. Tapping Daisy's hind quarters smartly, he said, "Get up, lazybones! The Sabbath will be upon us and you will not be milked."

The cow rolled her eyes at him, got up with a grunt, and started down the homeward path. When Tim had put Daisy in the cowpen, Granny came out to milk. She tucked up her plain skirts, sat on a three-legged stool, and while she milked gave Tim directions about Sabbath preparation.

"There is enough wood by the doorway, but the kindling box is empty. Be sure to fetch an extra pail of water for Sabbath needs." All the while the milk squirted in a muffled stream into the pail.

"Yes, Granny." Tim loved Granny Tetlow like a mother. His own mother had died when he was a baby.

Tim would get Lucy before he started his other tasks. He stopped under the early apple tree to fill his pockets. Munching an apple as he went, he followed the pathway into the woodland behind their cottage. The little bay mare whinnied expectantly when she saw him coming. She trotted to him, nuzzling him with her velvety nose, and nipping playfully at his lumpy pockets. Tim teased her a little, then gave her an apple.

Tangling his hand in the mare's thick mane, he led her to a stump and swung to her bare back. Bending to her ear, he urged her to a brisk canter. He liked to ride and was quite skillful on small Lucy's back. At home, Tim tethered her to a sapling near the shed, wishing all the time that he might go riding away, away off somewhere — he and Lucy! The Tinker sometimes rode the little mare to other towns, up and down the countryside, carrying his tools for mending in a bag hung from his saddle.

Granny had long since finished milking when Tim went to the spring for the pail of water. He filled the clumsy wooden pail with the gourd dipper and lugged it along the path to the cottage. The water splashed over his bare feet. It felt good.

Tim was panting, and the water was rocking in the pail as he reached the doorway. When he put it on the bench, some spilled over on Granny's freshly scrubbed floor. The boy rubbed his foot across the spatter, looking sidewise at Granny.

The little old lady, busily stirring something in a pot over the fire, paid no attention. Tim sniffed at the bitter smell that filled the room. Herb tea — it was what Granny had given him when he had chills and fever! Tim wrinkled his freckled nose, remembering how dreadful it had tasted.

Since he felt quite well, except for a lonesome ache, which no herb tea could help, Tim decided to leave at once. He was tiptoeing toward the door when Granny turned.

She said, "I need you, Timothy." Granny was the only person who called him Timothy. "The Whitcomb baby is sick as can be — poor little tyke, without a mother! Young Betsy is but sixteen and knows little about sickness." Granny began to pour the medicine through a cloth into a wooden bowl. "I need you to help me carry."

Tim felt better since the herb tea was going to the Whitcombs. He watched the last of the tea trickle through the cloth. "I hope the witches have not cast a spell on the baby, so it dies like good Dame Whitcomb did," he said.

Granny set the pot down with a thump. "Timothy, where did you hear such foolishness?" Granny's voice was sharp. It was usually soft and low.

"Ethan and John said she died because she was bewitched." Now it was out, the thing that had been troubling him all afternoon.

The smile crinkles left Granny's eyes and settled into worry wrinkles between her eyebrows. She laid her hand gently on Tim's shoulder. "Lad, witches are only in tales of fancy to tell by the fireside and quake at in jest. The Whitcomb baby's mother was not bewitched. She died of a sickness my herb tea would not cure."

Tim stared at her. "Are there not many witches shut in the jail? John said — "

The emphatic shake of Granny's head stopped him. "There are no witches in Salem to do harm to their fellow men."

Then Granny told him how the whole sorry matter began. Granny said that some girls, listening to the witch tales told by a West Indian servant in one of their homes, began to imagine they were bewitched. They made up strange tales of things they pretended to see. They cried out wildly, accusing this and that person of being a witch. The magistrates believed them, and began to arrest people for witchcraft. Anyone who had an enemy, or a grievance against a person, might accuse that person of witchcraft. Now the jail was filled with innocent people.

"But did they not hang witches on Gallows Hill last week?" Tim could not get the terrible day out of his mind.

Granny's blue eyes blazed. "For shame that such wrong is being done in Salem!"

Granny was wise and kind. She must be right, yet he could not forget the words of John and Ethan.

Tim watched Granny take a bowl from a shelf and fill it with milk. The Whitcombs had no cow.

Granny carried the herb tea, and Tim the milk. Betsy met them at the door. As soon as his hands were empty, Tim went in search of Dorcas. Dorcas was only a girl, but she was willing to play when the boys would not. She had even played Indian with him.

[15]

He found her by the tall hollyhocks in a corner of the garden. "Look, Tim! See my hollyhock ladies ready for church?" Dorcas pointed to a row of upside-down blooms.

They did look like gay ladies, Tim thought. "They are much too gaudy to go to church," he objected. "No one wears such finery or bright colors."

Dorcas pouted. "But we will only be playing. It would be so jolly to have a pretty silken dress." She smoothed her skirt of coarse homespun wistfully. All at once the dimples dented her cheeks again. "I know — we could have a ball for my hollyhock ladies. I have heard tell that great dames go to balls in fine silks that stand out like this!" She held up a red bloom, smiling at Tim. "Our ball would be only play!" she coaxed.

Tim grinned in spite of himself. "I can sing a merry tune I learned from Father. Listen!" He threw back his head and sang a song so rollicking that the hollyhocks seemed to sway to it.

Louder and louder he sang. Dorcas caught up two of the hollyhock dolls and danced them around wildly. Her brown curls fell from beneath

her white cap and bounced on her neckerchief.

So absorbed were they that they did not see the man with the solemn, scowling face peering at them from behind the snowball bush. He strode toward them, his face purple with rage, a switch in his hand. "Halt this wickedness!" he roared, "you children of the Evil One, profaning the Sabbath!" He brought the switch down in stinging blows across Tim's shoulders, once, twice, three times. Tim cringed, but did not cry out.

But when the tithing man moved toward Dor-

[17]

cas, who was standing quite still, the hollyhock blooms crushed in her clenched hands, Tim sprang forward. "No — no! Don't hit her. It was my fault, for I sang the merry song."

"Then you must take the punishment!" The stinging whip came down again and again across Tim's shoulders.

Tears were running down Dorcas's cheeks. "You are cruel!" she cried out. "It was a harmless thing we were doing."

"You, maid, act as if you were bewitched!" the man accused.

"Witches, bah! There are no witches except in fairy tales. Granny says so!" Tim shouted defiantly.

"So Granny Tetlow says there are no witches! The magistrate shall hear of this. Now, go to your homes, and do not show your faces until the church bell sounds tomorrow morning," the man growled.

Tim watched the broken hollyhock blooms fall from Dorcas's hands as she ran toward the cottage. Then he turned and fled.

[18]

2. The Sabbath Day

THE next morning Tim awoke at Granny's call. He blinked his eyes open, turned on the feather bed and stretched. His shoulders hurt. Then he remembered the sting of the tithing man's switch, and that it was the Sabbath. Reaching around his shoulders, he gingerly felt the sore spots.

He had told neither Granny nor the Tinker about his encounter with the tithing man the afternoon before. It would only have worried them.

Tim resolved to be very careful not to displease any tithing man today.

"Timothy! Timothy! Get up, lad, it is the Sabbath," Granny called again from below.

"Coming, Granny," Tim answered.

He started to plump up his feather bed and straighten his counterpane, but stopped still. There could be no bedmaking on the Sabbath. He climbed down the ladder from the loft, trying not to twitch his sore muscles.

"Come eat your mush and milk, Timothy, or we will be late for meeting," Granny prompted.

"Yes, Granny."

The boy ate quietly. As he drank a cup of Daisy's milk, he thought about yesterday and the Whitcomb baby. "Did the Whitcomb baby get well, Granny?" he asked between mouthfuls.

"It was quite pert when I left yesterday. The poor little tyke went right to sleep after I gave it the herb tea and milk." A little smile crinkled Granny's face. "Do you know, I think the milk did that baby as much good as my herb tea."

Tim grinned at her, then said thoughtfully, "If I would tend Daisy in the pasture to see that she eats well, would she give enough milk for us and the Whitcombs, too?"

"You might talk to Daisy about it," Tim's father suggested, quirking an eyebrow comically at Tim.

Tim laughed. "I might say, 'Daisy, eat more green grass, to make more white milk, because — ' "

Granny cut him short. "Such nonsense — and on the Sabbath, too," she tried to scold, working hard to pull her face into a solemn look. "Eat your breakfast," she admonished.

Tim still found it hard to keep from laughing as he walked sedately between the Tinker and Granny to the meetinghouse. In the churchyard, a tithing man was keeping a sharp watch over the boys waiting to go inside to the boys' pew. Tim saw Ethan nudge John and whisper in his ear behind the man's back. They edged away from Tim, leaving him next to Josiah Strong, who was a troublemaker. Tim wished heartily that their

[21]

keeper would take his eyes off him, so he could slide over to another place.

A feeling of loneliness took hold of Tim. On other Sabbaths it had been comforting to have John and Ethan near, though they could say nothing. Secretly they would nudge each other, and argue afterward about which one wanted to laugh most.

Just as he feared, Tim was beside Josiah when they filed into the pew. Then later, in the middle of a long prayer, something suddenly, painfully pinched Tim through his breeches leg. Without meaning to, he bounced up in the air with a hoarse shriek. He came down with a clatter on the hard body of a big lobster.

Next to him, Josiah sat with hands folded, eyes downcast, and an innocent expression on his red face. The tithing man's whip came down across Tim's sore shoulders with a swish. Tim gritted his teeth to keep from crying out again. Up and down the row of boys, hands went over mouths to choke their laughter.

"A-ha!" the man cried. Lifting the clinging

shellfish with his rod, he tried to carry it away with dignity.

"For shame that you would know no better than to carry such as that to meeting!" Josiah whispered.

"I did not — you know I did not," Tim denied under his breath.

"Serves you right that it pinched you," Tim's tormentor murmured.

Tim thought the morning service would surely go on forever and ever. He had never been so unhappy in his life. When noon recess came at last, he walked outside and let his breath out in a big sigh.

His throat was aching dry. Ethan and John were at the well before him, but he went on toward them, wondering what they would do. When they saw him coming, they let the bucket fall back into the well with a splash, and scurried away. If they would only talk to him!

The Tinker came to help him draw water. Taking turns, they drank deeply of the cold water from the gourd dipper kept by the well.

His father said nothing until Tim hung the dipper back on the tree. "What made you cry out in meeting, lad?" he asked softly, laying his hand on Tim's shoulder. Tim winced.

"There was a big lobster in the pew and it pinched me. Josiah Strong must have put it there, but the tithing man blames me, because yesterday —" Tim bit his lip and frowned down at his Sabbath shoes.

The Tinker looked at his son gravely. "What of yesterday?" he prompted.

Tim took a long breath. "At Whitcombs', I was singing one of our merry tunes, while Dorcas was dancing her hollyhock dolls. I did not know that the Sabbath was here, I declare I did not! A tithing man heard and switched me soundly."

Tim's father said nothing at first. Stealing a glance at him, Tim saw he was pulling an ear and staring into space. He did that when he was worried. At last he said, "This is a misfortune for us. Try to remember, lad, that we must walk carefully."

All at once Tim knew that some danger threatened their family. He could neither understand why nor tell exactly what it was. Witches had something to do with it, he was sure. And he had the uncomfortable feeling that he had made matters worse, by bringing the ill will of the tithing man upon him.

His father broke into his thoughts. "Come, Granny will be looking for us."

Granny had taken their noon lunch to the shade of a big tree. The Whitcombs were there, too. Betsy was feeding Baby Hugh cornbread soaked in water.

"Apple pulp would be good for the baby," Granny said, picking the softest red apple from those in the basket.

The Tinker reached into his pocket and drew out his jackknife. Taking the apple, he scraped it to a smooth uncooked sauce for the baby. Every time Tim saw his father use this fine knife, he wondered if he would ever own one like it. You could do marvelous things with a good jackknife! He was thinking so hard that he did not notice when Dorcas came to sit beside him.

He jumped when she whispered, "You were brave yesterday, Tim!"

His heart warmed at her praise. Boys were jolly, but girls were nice, too. If John and Ethan would not be friends, Dorcas would. But he only said, "It was wrong for me to anger the tithing man."

"If I had not wanted to play that we were having a grand ball for my hollyhock dolls, the tithing man would not have switched you," she whispered again.

"Oh, it was not your fault. Father taught me to tell time by the sun, and I should have known it was past three," Tim murmured gallantly.

They could talk no more then, for a deacon came to read them all a sermon while they were nooning. After that they went back to the hot meetinghouse for the afternoon preaching, psalm singing and more long prayers. Josiah leered at him and the other boys grinned, as they took their places in the boys' section. John and Ethan looked steadily in another direction.

At last the Sabbath service was over. The minister and his plain wife walked out of the church,

[26]

and then they were all free to go. Tim no longer had to pinch himself to keep awake. Even in his stiff leather shoes, it was hard to make his feet walk, not run, on the way home.

It was gray dusk by the time Tim found Daisy grazing at the edge of the woods, and brought her to be milked. He held the pineknot torch, which Granny lit for him, while the Tinker milked. Lucy whinnied somewhere off in the woods. They missed each other on the Sabbath when Tim could not ride the little bay mare.

When they took the milk in, the Tinker looked at Granny and moved his head in the direction of the woods, lifting his eyebrows. Granny nodded, and the Tinker went hastily out. Lately, he was often gone during the evening. Sometimes Tim would waken when his father came home, to hear him talking with Granny in low, earnest tones, in the room below. Dozing off again, he would not hear his father come to bed.

Granny strained the warm milk through a cloth, then dipped a cupful for him. It tasted fresh and sweet.

[27]

"Baby Hugh and Dorcas would like some, wouldn't they, Granny?" Tim said.

"That they would, Timothy." Little Granny was stepping briskly about, stirring the fire to heat water for dishwashing. "But I must be here when your father returns."

Forgetting the night noises of prowling wild animals, and the deep shadows along the uneven path to the Whitcomb cottage, Tim offered eagerly, "I will take it."

Granny smiled at him quizzically. "The moon is only coming up. It will not light the path."

"I want to go, Granny! I do want to!" he coaxed with shining eyes.

"You will not be afraid, lad?"

"But, Granny, you always say that a wise Divine Providence watches over us," Tim reminded.

"So He does, lad." As she laid her hand caressingly on his sore shoulder, Tim flinched.

Granny looked at him searchingly. "All day I have noticed that your shoulders were touchy. Off with that jacket!"

Hesitatingly, Tim pulled it off. Red welts stood

[28]

up on his white skin. Granny clicked her tongue, shaking her head. "Now, tell me about it."

While Granny brought her healing ointment and bathed the welts, Tim told her about the tithing man, about the hollyhock dolls, ball, and the lobster in the pew.

"It is a fine pass we have come to when a child cannot play — " She stopped, sighing deeply. "But do try, Timothy, not to break the laws."

"Yes, Granny." Timothy wiggled. "You tickle. Is that not enough ointment? Do I go?"

"Perhaps." Tim's eyes widened as Granny took her crockery jar with the pewter lid from the shelf, and began to fill it with milk. Tim had often heard Granny tell how her mother had brought it from England. He would have to be truly careful of it, for Granny prized it. "It will be easier to carry than a bowl in the dark," she explained.

The starlight was pale and the bushes were thick along the way. Tim looked back to see Granny put a candle in the window. He held the precious jar against his thumping heart. After a bit he passed

[29]

the crossing of an old Indian trail that led westward. Several times he had ridden Lucy along the
trodden path, but not far, lest he get lost in the
wilderness, or meet wild beasts.

Tim found the door of the Whitcomb house
closed and bolted. A candle burned inside. Since
his hands were full, he kicked the door lightly.
There was a scurrying about within, and at last
Betsy's scared voice called, "Who is there?"

"It is only Tim with milk for the baby."

Betsy unbolted the door, peered through a
crack, then flung it open. "Oh, I am glad it is
only you, Tim!" she breathed. "I know not what
to expect — the town officers might come, and
Father is away."

So their father was away, too! Tim wished he
knew where, for perhaps the Tinker was there,
too.

While Betsy was emptying the milk, Dorcas's
nightcapped head appeared at the top of the
crooked narrow stairway. "Tim, you are brave
to come alone," she said with wide eyes.

Dorcas had called him brave twice. John and

Ethan had never called him brave. Sometimes they teased him about being afraid to climb as high as they did.

Tim looked up at Dorcas, swaggering a little. "There is nothing to be afraid of!" he grinned.

"Go back to bed, like a good little maid," Betsy wheedled. "I will bring you a cup of the fresh milk presently."

Tim took the empty jar, thinking how pretty it was, with the crown traced on the lid and the colored design on the side. He felt unafraid as he started homeward. Picking his way lest he stub his toe and fall, he gripped the jar tightly. The moon was still low in the east.

Just before he reached the crossing of the Indian trail, he heard the sound of muffled hoofbeats. He hastened to hide behind a bush at the crossing. Who could be riding so fast in the dark?

As he watched, a large dark horse swept by, silhouetted in the moonlight that shone across an open space. A big man urged him on; a woman rode behind him, her long dark cloak flying in the breeze. Tim shuddered. Witches rode broom-

[31]

sticks, according to the tales, but perhaps they would claim a ride on a horse, too!

The first horse was not out of sound when another came along the path toward him. This one was smaller, as was her rider. All at once Tim knew the gait of the little horse. He stepped forward. "Lucy!" he cried out. She swerved, scraping the bushes beside him.

A swaying branch caught Granny's jar from his hands and dashed it to the ground in a dozen broken fragments. The little mare whinnied back at him. But there was a woman wrapped in a dark, billowing cloak behind her rider, and Lucy could not stop!

With a choking sob of fear and dismay, his hands shaking, Tim fumbled at the broken pieces of pottery in the dark. Finally, he gave up and started along the path home, his throat aching with dry sobs, one hand clutching a piece of the broken jar.

3. The Jackknife

Granny's candle threw a faint light across the path, as Tim neared the house. The door was open for him. He could hear the Tinker and Granny talking in low tones. The boy stopped in the doorway, surprised that his father was there. It had been a small man, about his father's size, who had been riding Lucy!

Then he stumbled across the threshold holding out the piece of crockery jar, his lip quivering in a way to make the boys of Salem scoff. Even Dorcas could not have called him brave!

"See, Granny, see! I broke your pretty jar. And a witch has run away with Lucy," he mumbled in a strange singsong voice.

Granny turned startled eyes on him. "Whatever are you talking about, Timothy? Are you sick? Are you coming down with chills and fever again —and out of your mind?" She went over and laid her hand on his forehead, puckering her face anxiously. "You are hot with fever, lad. I am going to put you to bed, right here in this room!"

Tim lay down on the little bed in the corner where Granny slept. The Tinker came to him, gently loosening his fingers from the piece of jar.

"It is a good thing the witch-hunters of Salem cannot see you now, lad, for they would surely say you were bewitched, so scared you are about nothing," the Tinker joked, trying to cheer him.

Granny stirred the fire until it blazed. She brought a pot, making quite a clatter. "Do not fret about the jar, Timothy," she comforted him. "Now, I am going to brew you some herb tea."

Tim's father brought a fresh log and put it on the coals. Granny hung the pot to boil and went to fetch the herbs from the shed. When she came back, the Tinker closed the door and bolted it, saying, "The salt air from the sea is cool, even on a summer night."

But that was not what was making Tim shiver and shake. He could not get away from the sight he had seen on the Indian trail.

His father came to sit beside him. Seeing Tim shake, he tucked the counterpane more closely about his young son. As the pot began to boil, Tim's shaking stopped.

After a bit his father said, "Now tell us what scared you so tonight, lad. Why did you talk so strangely when you came in?"

All the quietness of the peaceful, familiar room left Tim again. "There were witches — I saw them! Two men rode the horses; the big man on the big horse, and the little man on Lucy. And there were the witches hanging on behind — I saw them with my own eyes! And they made Lucy jump and break the jar. I'll never see the

little bay mare again, for she has gone with the witches!" The tears began to run down Tim's flushed cheeks.

The Tinker and Granny exchanged glances. "Come, come, Tim," soothed his father. "No witch, were there such creatures, could ride that little bay mare of ours. Why, Lucy would throw her off as quick as lightning! Like this she would — "

His father pranced about the room, kicking

up his heels, and twisting his back in a comical fashion. Then Tim laughed. In his mind he could just picture spirited Lucy pitching the witch into the brush by the wayside.

But there, beyond his father's playful antics, a grim face was staring at them through the unbarred windows. It was the tithing man.

"Look!" Tim gasped. "Look! At the window!"

The Tinker stopped as if frozen in his shoes. Granny turned. Unheeded, her ladle dripped brown herb tea on the freshly scrubbed floor. The three of them watched motionless until the man slunk away from the window.

"Spying again! And what a case they could make of this in the court," the little man muttered, his forehead creased with worry.

Granny's hands were trembling. "Yes," she said through lips that had lost their color.

The Tinker sat down wearily on a bench beside Tim. Pulling an ear again, he began by and by to talk to Tim. "Listen, lad, time and again Granny and I have told you that there are no real witches. Those who accuse people of being witches are doing great wickedness. Innocent people of Salem have been hanged, because other people have sworn things to be true that never happened — imagined things." The Tinker shook his head sadly. "Some who pretended to be bewitched were children, yet the magistrates believed the false tales they told of horrible sights they never saw." Tim's father stared into the fire. "I hope our Tim will never be so foolish."

Tim drew a shuddering breath. "Oh, Father!" he protested.

His father went on. "This is how such terrible things can happen. Witches are said to brew evil potions in kettles, you know. Would you say Granny is a witch because she stirred your herb tea in a kettle?"

Tim sat straight up in bed, his eyes flashing blue fire. "Granny could not be an evil old witch! She is good and kind."

His father nodded solemnly. "Yet, someone peering in the window, seeing Granny making herb tea, might say that she was a witch." A tired little smile flicked across his face. "And seeing me, a grown man, capering around the room, kicking up my heels, and my small son lying sick in bed, they might say we were bewitched, if they had a mind to."

Now, Tim began to see what his father meant when he spoke of the case that could be made in court. But surely no one could accuse Granny of being a witch! She always went about the neighborhood helping people. Then, remembering the face at the window, Tim shivered.

The Tinker said softly, "Tim, can you keep a secret?" Tim's eyes searched his father's face in the dim candlelight. "Yes, Father, I promise."

"I think you should know this, so you will not worry about Lucy. She was carrying to safety a good woman, who was about to be falsely accused of witchcraft. A friend is riding with her to another province, where she will live until Salem people have come to their senses again."

"How long will Lucy be gone?" Tim could not help asking.

"Not long — two days perhaps. Another rider will meet them. Then Lucy's rider will bring her home. The big horse and his rider will return, too."

In spite of the danger that seemed to hang over them, Tim felt a kind of happiness surge up inside him. "Good little Lucy! Brave little Lucy," he said huskily.

Granny brought the herb tea in a pewter cup, and sat down beside Tim on the bed. Tim turned away, making a wry face. "Could I not have milk instead, Granny? See, I am quite all right again."

His grandmother put her hand on his forehead. "It is strange — the fever seems to have left."

The Tinker chuckled. "Your herb tea would cure anyone, Mother — just smelling it!"

But there was a firm look about her pleasant mouth. "Now that I made it, you will drink it." Her lips twitched a little. "It is good for many ailments, even being scared. I will bring you a cup of Daisy's milk to wash it down." So saying she bustled away to the cupboard.

With a gulp, Tim swallowed the tea, then reached eagerly for the cup of milk.

When Tim awoke in the morning the fearful events of the evening seemed far away. There was porridge in a pot over a smoldering fire in the big fireplace. He had on his jacket and was ready to eat when Granny came in from milking Daisy. It was still only gray dawn.

"As soon as you take Daisy to pasture, your father needs you to help in the workshop," Granny said, dishing up Tim's porridge and pouring fresh milk over it.

As he watched her, a great tenderness for her welled up in Tim. Suddenly he put his arms around her neck, hugging her hard.

"Now Timothy!" she pretended to scold. "You almost made me spill your milk." She straightened her cap and neckerchief.

Like most Puritan families, the Tetlows did not do much hugging and kissing. But Tim knew that when they were anxious about his being sick, and about his doing right, it was because Granny and the Tinker loved him.

"Granny," he mumbled around a mouthful of porridge, "tell me again about Aunt Susie Williams, Uncle Ezra's mill, Cousin Seth and Cousin Polly, and all the little cousins."

"How many times must I tell you?" Granny drawled in her soft voice. "Time and again I have told you how my daughter, Susanna, married Miller Williams and went away over to Worcester to live. And how I miss them! You are the only grandchild I have close enough to patch clothes for, and dose with herb tea when something ails you," she sighed.

Tim dawdled with his porridge, thinking. "If Seth and Polly were here, we could have jolly times," he said wistfully, longing for friends.

"Your father will give you a jolly time, if you do not get about your tasks," Granny reminded him.

Tim gulped his porridge then.

While driving Daisy to pasture, he wondered

if Lucy's rider would stop to graze and water her. Would he lash her? At a light touch, her feet would fly. He missed her early morning whinny.

Later, at the workshop, Tim found his father working on the wheel. Tim leaned against the workbench. "Is it a cart, Father?" Without waiting for a reply, he rattled on. "In it will you travel far beyond the towns where Lucy carried you?"

The Tinker complained fretfully, "Is it not enough that we have need of wheels, and soon? What you do not know, you cannot tell — if the authorities question you."

Silently Tim watched, as his father showed him how to smooth the spokes with a piece of leather in the sand trough. "Be diligent, lad. I must go to the fireside to burn out the holes in the rims and axles for the spokes."

Tim felt a small soreness of heart because his father did not trust him to know about the wheels. Was not Lucy's mission much more important than wheels, yet he had told him about that! But that was only to ease his foolish fears, of which he was now ashamed.

When the Tinker came to see how Tim was getting along, his praise made Tim's heart glad again. His father said with a twinkle, "How would you like to use a knife this afternoon?"

The Tinker laid his best jackknife on the workbench. Tim's face glowed. A few times he had been permitted to use an old knife, but this one — never! His father showed him how to whittle wooden pegs. They were to hold something together, Tim knew, but he must not ask what. He measured and smoothed them carefully, laying them in a neat pile.

By midafternoon Tim's hand was reddened and blistered, though he did not complain. But the Tinker saw him blow his breath on it and came to see.

"You have been faithful to your task, and you use the knife well. You deserve a holiday, only be back to fetch Daisy." He snapped the blade shut and laid the knife in Tim's hand. "It is time you had a knife of your own."

Tim gazed at it, hardly believing. No boy in Salem had a finer one. Stuffing it among the treasures in his pocket, he stammered his gratitude.

As he went down to the spring for a drink, he stopped to carve an inscription on a big tree. "Tim," he cut in the curving letters he had learned in the village school. Below he cut the date, "1692."

Now that this was done, what should he do next with his prized knife? If Ethan and John were friends — but a sudden thought sent him off at breakneck speed. They lived across town, John near the wharves, Ethan near his father's mill. On he ran.

A man in a broadbrim hat stepped from a doorway squarely into Tim's heedless path. Their collison sent the man's hat rolling in the dust. Tim looked at the man then — he was Quaker Heath! Quakers were not well thought of, for they did not go to the meetinghouse on the square.

"Had thee not better look where thee is going?" the man inquired mildly.

"I did not mean to — " Tim stammered, picking up the hat and brushing it off.

Quaker Heath's eyes twinkled at Tim. "I know

thee did not, lad. But suppose it had been a Puritan Father, that thee had dashed against?"

The big Quaker's smile surprised Tim. He had always thought him a solemn person. "I was hurrying to lend my knife to John and Ethan, so they would play with me again," Tim explained.

"It is sad when friends will not be friends," Quaker Heath said. Granny had said something quite like that! Then he asked, "Is thee not the Tinker's son?" Tim bobbed his head. "He is a fine man, and kindly."

"He gave me his best jackknife, and I know he did it because I am lonesome," Tim confided. "Now, if John and Ethan will only use it! For they have none as sharp."

"I wish thee success, lad. But be careful to walk circumspectly, for where would they find room in the overflowing jail for thee and me?"

At last, Tim reached the wharves. Out where the fishing boats docked, Tim saw the two boys — Ethan, tall and thin, hair rumpled; John, sturdy, roundheaded.

"Yoo-hoo!" Tim hailed them.

They turned and looked at him, then spoke together in low, excited tones.

"Don't come — don't you dare come any closer!" John yelled.

In spite of their warning, Tim reached confidently into his pocket and fished his knife from among the other things there. He opened the blade and flashed it in the sun. "See my new jackknife! You may use it if you want." Eagerly he took a few steps toward them, for surely now they would want to play again with him!

"He is bewitched! He has a knife to cut our throats!" Ethan shrieked.

"Stay away — Granny Tetlow is a witch, and she has bewitched you!" shouted John.

Ethan took up the cry, too. Together they chanted it, "Granny Tetlow is a witch! Granny Tetlow is a witch!"

The horror of it made Tim's stomach feel sick and empty at the same time. He looked at the knife. Drawing back his arm, he flung it from him as far as he could. Then he ran.

[48]

4. Granny Takes a Journey

TIM sped across town, caring not at all if a tithing man saw his pell-mell pace. His mind was in a dull unhappy whirl. His feet went up and down, up and down. Past the overcrowded jail, past the magistrate's house where trials were held, past the church he ran.

The whining song of Granny's spinning wheel filled the air as he neared the cottage. Through the door he could see her little figure, swaying in her high-backed chair, while she treadled and the spindle turned. Flinging himself across the room he sank down beside her, shaking with dry, aching sobs.

"They called you a witch, Granny!" he choked.

She put her arm across Tim's shoulders. "Who did?" she almost whispered. He could feel her tremble.

"John and Ethan! I wouldn't have them for friends — I wouldn't!" he cried angrily. "They are cruel! I hate them!"

"No, Timothy, no! You must never hate anyone. Hate only twists the mind and spoils the stomach for eating. But it is hard to have even the children calling out falsehoods about me." Her face was white, but her voice was low and slow as usual. "They have been misled. Surely the towns-people will get their wits back and see the wrong they are doing. Until then, we must be patient."

"What will they do to you, Granny — what will they do?" The boy gazed anxiously into her troubled face.

Granny only shook her head. "Go fetch your

[50]

father." She began to push her spinning wheel back into its corner.

The Tinker laid aside his work and listened gravely to his son. He sighed from deep inside him, when Tim had finished. "It has come, as I feared."

Tim followed his father silently to the house. Granny sat in her high-backed chair, her hands clasped in her lap. A sadness had settled on her pale face.

"Well, Mother, it has come," said the Tinker. "If the boys of the town are calling 'Witch!' it will not be long until the witch-hunters of Salem come to accuse you openly. You must leave to-night. I will go at once to make the plans."

"How will Granny go?" Tim asked.

"A friend will take Granny on his big horse," Tim's father replied, smiling at him quietly. Granny smiled, too, but the hand that smoothed her skirts trembled. Try though he did, Tim could not smile, for his face was stiff.

"Where will you go, Granny?" Tim wanted to know.

[51]

Granny looked at the Tinker, who shook his head. Granny's reply was not much help in quieting his misgiving. "Some day you will know all about it," she murmured.

Tim wiggled his bare toes, and watched them wiggle, to hide the disappointment in his eyes. He would not even know where Granny was at night. And how he would miss her at bedtime when he said his prayers.

The Tinker went out the door. Tim stood watching him go down the path that led into the woods, until he heard Granny begin to move about in the room. She brought a covered basket in which to carry her belongings. Tim remembered how he had helped her gather the reeds for that basket. He watched her fetch her simple clothes and put them into the basket. A painful lump rose in his throat.

"Granny, if I had not broken your pretty jar, you could take it along," Tim said huskily.

"Now, Timothy, I told you not to fret about that jar," reminded Granny. "I could not take it on horseback anyway."

"You treasured it highly," Tim persisted. "And someday I will find another like it for you." Making this promise gave him comfort.

His father came back presently, looking quite cheerful. Casting about, his eyes came to rest on the water pail. "Tim, I think we should have another pail of water from the spring," he said.

Tim looked sorrowfully at his family, for the pail was half full. It was plain they wanted him out of earshot when they talked of Granny's going. He knew that he was not to know where Granny was bound for. Maybe he would not even know when she went. She might be gone when he returned!

On his way to the spring, Tim poured the water out on the vegetable bed. When he came back, lugging the heavy pail, his father was leaving the cottage for the workshop. To his great relief, his grandmother was still there, putting the room in order.

"I was afraid you would leave while I was gone," he cried out breathlessly, setting the water on the bench.

[53]

A shadow of a smile crossed Granny's face. "Witches cannot ride until after sundown, lad."

Tim grinned back at her. If she could make a jest of the journey, perhaps she was not going away forever.

"You are to go to the workshop. Your father needs you." She prodded the fire, then dampened a finger on her tongue to test the heat of the fireplace oven. Tim hoped she was going to make puff apple pie.

In the workshop Tim found his father working furiously, pegging together pieces of wood to make a sort of box. It must be a cart-bed, Tim thought, but knew better than to ask again.

"Let me see your hands, Tim." Tim opened them obediently. "Are they too sore for you to use your jackknife?"

Tim stood in stunned silence. He had not told his father that in his anger he had thrown the knife away. He could not tell him now, for he would think — he could not help but think — that Tim had not prized the fine knife.

"I — I do not have the knife," Tim muttered

under his breath. He stared hard at the pile of shavings to keep from meeting his father's gaze.

"You do not have it?" The Tinker eyed him searchingly. "Surely you have not lost it so soon!"

Tim's eyes went fleetingly to his father's face in a beseeching look, then back to his toes pushing shavings about. Then he told his first real falsehood. "Yes — I lost it." Was it not better to let his father think he had lost it than to tell him he had thrown it away in anger?

His father was silent for so long that Tim stole another glance at him. It hurt to see the disappointed look on his face.

The Tinker sighed. "You may use this knife, though it is not half so keen as the one I gave you."

Without a word, Tim took the knife and began to whittle out more of the little wooden pegs, which his father was using. He was patient when his father corrected his work, showing him how to round and smooth the hard wood. Nor did Tim ask any questions when his father pulled back the piece of sailcloth, uncovering the two wheels, complete but for the iron on the rims. A pair of shafts, fashioned from saplings which had bent just right in growing, were there, too.

As the hot afternoon wore on, the sweat rolled from their faces. Tim was weary, but much worse was his heartache. He thought hard, trying to find a way to explain to his father about the falsehood he had told, but he was sure he could not make him understand.

Before they knew it, the afternoon was gone and the sun was sinking low behind the woods to the west.

"You helped well, Tim," his father said.

The praise pleased him, but the thought of his falsehood still bothered him. Perhaps now, when his father thought well of him, would be a good time to tell about the jackknife. But the words would not come.

Granny came to the door of the cottage then and called, "Timothy! It is time to fetch Daisy."

"Yes, Granny." Tomorrow Granny would not be here. There would only be the Tinker and himself. He could hardly bear it.

Tim trotted along the path to the pasture. He

wanted to be with Granny all the time he could until she left them. Daisy was unusually slow. The air was heavy with the promise of rain, and the flies tormented her even more than usual. She stopped often to throw her head back across her spotted shoulders, slapping at the biting insects with her wet tongue. Her tail flapped ceaselessly, and she did not seem to mind Tim's switch. He gave her a harder whack.

"One would think you were bewitched," he snapped crossly.

After a seemingly endless length of time, he turned the cow into the cowpen. Granny came briskly with the milk pail.

Suddenly a clear, eager neighing sounded from the woods. Lucy was back! Stopping only long enough to pick up some apples from the ground and stuff them into his pocket, Tim ran in the direction of the little mare's call. The pathway was already shadowy, but Tim could see a man dragging a saddle from Lucy's back. When he came closer he saw it was Mr. Whitcomb. So that was why he was away from home!

Lucy's head drooped. Her flanks were trembling. She nuzzled her nose against Tim, feeling for apples. Without teasing her, Tim gave her one and stood fondling her.

"No finer little mare ever traveled the wilderness trails," said Tim's neighbor. "She may have saved a life by her steady, fast gait, for the innocent woman she carried is far from her accusers. Now, I must not be seen with this saddle." And Mr. Whitcomb hurried to take it to the workshop, where it was kept.

With pride Tim stroked the little bay mare, wishing that Granny could ride away on her. He led her to the stream and stood by while she drank deeply. Gathering large dock leaves, he wet them in the brook, and bathed the tired little mare's lathered coat. Then he turned her loose in the wood to graze.

The thought of Granny's going sent his feet flying back to the cottage. Granny smiled fondly at him when he came in.

She said cheerfully, "I baked puff apple pie. There will be enough for tomorrow."

Watching her set his favorite dish on the plank table, Tim wondered how long it would be before she baked him another. He went to wash up in the wooden bowl near the door.

"Lucy is home," he said through a faceful of water.

"The little mare must be spent." Granny's voice was full of compassion.

The Tinker came in. Tim stood, as usual, near the table while his father said grace. He shut his eyes tight, so as not to look at the apple pie. Yet, when it came to eating he could hardly swallow. The vegetable stew would scarcely go past the lump in his throat. And how anything as good as the pie could refuse to go down was past his thinking.

After supper Granny washed the dishes and Tim carried them to the shelves. Tim's eyes followed her about the familiar tasks.

She turned anxious eyes on her son. "Do you not think it best that Timothy go with us, instead of staying in the house? Should the authorities come, the lad would not know what to answer."

"You are right, Mother," he agreed. "I have begun to fret about your journey, for I fear there is a storm brewing."

Soon thunder began to rumble in the distance. When the Tinker went to the door, Tim crept up beside him. Black clouds were rolling in rapidly from the sea.

"Granny cannot go in a storm, can she?" Tim asked hopefully.

"Better in a storm than in jail," Tim's father said grimly. "We must start, for there is no telling when the authorities will be upon us."

The Tinker walked ahead, carrying Granny's light basket. Granny followed, with Tim at her heels.

Already the wind was lashing and bending the trees. Drops of rain, as big as beads, began pelting them. Except when lightning flashed, the path was in deep gloom. One great limb of a tree crashed to the ground before them.

After a bit, the Tinker led them into a branching path. By now they were drenched with rain. On and on they plodded — for miles, it seemed to

Tim. The thunder was rolling away in the distance, the lightning was feeble, and the roar of the wind had died down, when they came to an old woodland thatched cottage. It looked deserted.

Granny stooped to wring the water from her clinging skirts, while the Tinker knocked a strange signal on the weather-beaten door. When the door opened cautiously, Tim gaped in surprise. It was Quaker Heath standing there.

"Is thee ready?" the big man asked Granny.

"Yes," said Granny, giving her skirts a little shake. Seeing the concern on their faces she tried to smile. "They will dry on the way."

Quaker Heath led his big black horse from behind the cottage. Granny put her arm across Tim's wet shoulders and kissed his cheek. "Be a good lad," she said.

"Good-by, Granny." Tim would not cry, or hug her tight as he wanted to, lest it not be manly. But his throat was about to burst with the lump there.

Quaker Heath swung to the saddle. The Tinker hoisted Granny to the pillion behind him. Quaker Heath said to Tim, "Be a brave lad."

[61]

And they were off down the leaf-padded wilderness trail, the late dusk of the summer day swallowing them.

With each homeward step Tim took, something inside him kept saying, "Be brave, be good — be brave, be good."

When they reached home, he helped his father bring the parts of the cart to the cottage. By then darkness had fallen. The Tinker barred both the door and windows securely. By the light of a candle, set on the table-board, and a pineknot torch on the hearth, the Tinker worked. Tim helped what little he could.

Tim's father talked as he worked. "You have been patient, lad, and deserve to know what we will do. When the cart is finished, perhaps tomorrow, we will go vagabonding together. There is much tinkering to be done about the countryside."

"Will Lucy take us? Will we have friends on the way?" Tim's eyes were full of eager questions.

"Yes, Lad. There are many people with kind hearts. 'Tis a fine land. If God had not liked a merry song, He would not have made the birds to sing. Had He not liked beauty, He would not have made the flowers and trees. If He wanted people to be cruel and stern, He would have made their hearts of stone."

The Tinker had scarcely ceased speaking when there came a thunderous pounding on the door. Not moving, scarcely breathing, Tim watched his father go to the door and unbar it. There stood four men.

A burly man standing in front said, "In the name of the law, we come to take one who bewitches even her own family!"

"Your talk of witches is childish prattle. You throw innocent people into jail and hang them from the gallows," the Tinker said with dignity.

The man's face turned blueberry purple. The mouths of the men behind him hung open at the Tinker's daring. Tim thrilled at his father's courage.

"Aside!" their leader roared.

Tim's father came to stand beside his son. That gave Tim courage, too.

The men swarmed over the cottage, up to the attic, beating the feather beds and moving the furniture about. After looking in every nook and cranny, they finally gave up.

"So, she got away! Left on a broomstick, no doubt," the burly man snarled. "But she'll be brought to justice, you'll see! And look well to yourself, Tinker, daring to deny the being of witches. Doubtless, you are one yourself!"

The men went stormily out the door and stamped away into the night.

The Tinker closed the door gently and barred it. The sound of the men's feet died away.

5. Unhappiness Is Everywhere

TIM stirred uneasily. "Will they come back, Father?"

The Tinker brushed a weary hand across his forehead. "We will be safe for a few hours from their prying, I would judge. But we must hasten to leave Salem." He sighed as he said, "Bedtime, Tim."

Obediently Tim climbed the ladder to the loft. But he could not sleep. Presently he heard the ringing of the curfew bell, and knew it was nine o'clock. He was chock-full of questions about Granny. Saying his prayers without her had seemed impossible, so he had crawled into bed without praying. That troubled him. Then, too, he had meant to tell his father about the knife.

The light from the pineknot torch flickered into the attic at the ladder opening. He could hear the scrape of his father's tools on wood, the tap of his mallet. He slid from bed and crept over to peer down at his father's tired figure.

Fathers were expected to be stern, but the Tinker did not look so, down there in the dancing light. At last he ventured, "Father, I am so lonely up here."

His father straightened, wiped the sweat from his face with his sleeve, and looked up at Tim. "Very well, come down. It is lonely down here, too."

Tim lost no time drawing close to his father. "Do they have fast horses? Will they find Granny, do you think?" he questioned.

"Fast horses going in the wrong direction can

be of no use, lad." The little smile on the Tinker's face eased Tim's fears.

"Will we start being vagabonds tomorrow, do you think?" Usually Tim would not have asked questions so boldly. But tonight was different.

"Tomorrow — if the watchman does not see my light and halt my work, we will take the wheels to my friend, the blacksmith, to have the iron put on. Then there will be a little work yet to be done." Tim's father glanced anxiously at the barred windows.

"He is your friend? I did not know we had a friend, but the Whitcombs — and Quaker Heath," Tim sighed.

"We have many friends. But they too fear the harsh ways of Salem. Someday, though, it will be much better."

"Why is Quaker Heath our friend, Father? He does not go to the Puritan meetinghouse, but to the Quaker meetinghouse."

"He is our friend because he has love in his heart. The strange part, lad, is that our fathers came to this fair land that they might live and worship as their hearts said. Now, their sons have forgotten that freedom must be for all. But this will be a land of freedom yet."

Tim listened gravely, thinking it out for himself. It meant that, if you had love in your heart, you would not be too eager for your own way in all things.

Now was the time to tell his father about the jackknife. He squared his shoulders and began. "Father, I told a falsehood. I did not lose the jackknife. I was angry because John and Ethan said I would cut their throats with it, and I threw it away. It was foolish and wasteful."

For an anxious moment his father did not speak. Then he said, "It was a thoughtless thing to do." But to soften his reproach, he laid a soothing hand on Tim's shoulder. "Perhaps you can find it yet. If not, it may serve to make you think before you act."

The boy drew a deep breath of relief. His father was not angry!

The hot room, the sound of his father working, and the late hour made Tim begin to nod sleepily.

His father started to carry him to Granny's little bed in the corner. He roused, saying drowsily, "I — did not say my prayers — because Granny was not here."

The Tinker regarded him gravely. "God is as close as when Granny is here. We ought always to pray."

Together they knelt by the little bed. Tim said his prayer. His father asked God to watch over Granny, and to make them all brave in danger, and thoughtful of others at all times. His mind at rest, his body weary, Tim slept soundly.

Long before dawn, the Tinker awakened him. They went to the cowpen, where Tim held the pineknot torch while his father milked.

"Whatever will become of Daisy when we are vagabonding?" Tim asked anxiously.

"The Whitcombs are pleased to give her care for her milk, while we are gone," his father assured him.

Tim was glad that little Hugh was to have Daisy's milk. Dorcas liked milk, too.

After breakfast the Tinker, carrying the cart

wheels, led the way through bypaths skirting the village to the smithy. The shop was near the wharf, for there was much work to be done for the shipbuilders, as well as the shoeing of horses. The blacksmith was waiting for them and the coals were glowing in the forge. He had already been at work, and had partly made the iron pieces for the wheels. Tim stood watching the sparks fly from under the brawny man's hammer, as he and John and Ethan had often done when they were given a holiday from tasks.

When the dawn came creeping over the earth, Tim thought of his jackknife. "Father, may I go look for my knife now?" he asked.

"Lose it?" asked the smith, looking up from his work.

The Tinker told him of Tim's meeting with the boys on the wharf, which had warned them that it was time for Granny to flee. Tim ran down to the wharf. He tried to think where he had stood, which way he had flung the knife. He crawled on his hands and knees, searching in the cracks of the roughhewn planks, but he could not find it.

He could not hope to see it again. And what a prize it would be for the finder!

Downhearted, he went back to the smithy. His father was ready to go home, and the friendly smith had offered to bring the wheels when they were done.

When they reached home, Daisy was lowing to be off to the pasture. Tim hurried her along to the meadows, for the Tinker had promised that he could take milk to the Whitcombs. So full of news was he that he could hardly wait to see their good neighbors.

The Whitcomb door was open to the morning sunshine. Betsy saw him, laid the baby in the crib, and came to take the milk. Dorcas sat sewing, her pretty face screwed up seriously over her work.

"How is Granny's health this fine morning?" Betsy inquired politely.

"Granny has gone." How sad it sounded, Tim thought.

"Gone! When? Did anything awful happen?" Betsy's startled voice plied him with questions, her sweet face puckered with worry.

[72]

Dorcas dropped her work and ran to stare at Tim. "Where did she go?"

"Father will not say. Halfway round the world, maybe." Thinking of Granny half a world away was dreadful. But Dorcas's wide eyes had prompted him to make Granny's flight sound like a great adventure. "She went in the storm," he added.

"What made her go so suddenly?" Betsy puzzled.

"It was John and Ethan shouting that she was a witch, that made Father know that it was time for Granny to go. They screeched that I was bewitched, and would cut their throats with my jackknife Father gave me. I only meant to lend it to them."

Betsy sighed. "I wish her safe."

"After the storm, the searchers came and turned the house topsy-turvy. They were angry, and said they would bring Granny to trial. But they will not find her," Tim told them confidently.

Betsy's face was solemn as she went to warm some milk for Baby Hugh.

[73]

Tim went close to Dorcas. "Can you keep a secret?"

Dorcas's cheeks dimpled. "Oh, yes, Tim! What is it?" She pushed her cap and curls off an ear and bent toward him.

"Father and I are going to be vagabonds. We will travel about the country with Lucy pulling a cart that Father and I have made — at least I helped a little with the making. Father will tinker, and I — well, perhaps I can earn enough to buy Granny another jar like the one I broke," Tim confided. Then he added wistfully, "If I can find one."

Dorcas's shoulders drooped. "Oh, Tim! I do not want you to go away!" she wailed. "I will have no one to play with at all."

Tim cast about in his mind for a way to comfort her. "Dorcas, I will look for the biggest holly-hocks in all the countryside. I will bring you the seed to plant, then you will have the biggest holly-hock dolls in the land." Tim measured a great circle vaguely with his roughened hands.

Dorcas laughed merrily. "There are no hollyhocks so big, Tim!" Her face sobered. "I will miss you, Tim." She reached out and patted his hand.

Tim tried to console her further. "You will have all Daisy's milk until we come home. Father has already told your father so."

Dorcas jumped up and down. "I must tell Betsy everything! She will be glad about Daisy!" And she started to run in search of Betsy. Tim bounced after her. Catching her roughly by the shoulder he whirled her about. "No — no! You must not tell our secret!"

Dorcas jerked away from him. "You are cruel!" Her lips began to tremble. "What good is a secret if you cannot share it?"

Tim scowled at her. "Humph! It is no secret if you tell it. I'll tell you nothing else at all — nothing at all, for you cannot be trusted!"

He started on the run for home. Once he turned, to see Dorcas standing still, her face stricken and white. He had not meant to quarrel. Before he left he must tell her so.

It was near noon when he heard the hoofbeats of horses approaching. Hiding behind the lilac bush, Tim watched the riders pass. The horses were lathered with sweat; the men slouched in their saddles, their faces sullen. They were the searchers of the night before. And they did not have Granny!

The boy caught his breath and scurried toward the workshop. The blacksmith had brought the wheels and was helping the Tinker fasten them on the axletree of the cart. They looked up when Tim made his headlong appearance, stubbing his toe on the door-piece.

"Haste makes waste, lad. I venture to say you will have a sore toe." The blacksmith stood grinning at him.

Tim looked down at his toe to see the blood beginning to run. But he did not care. "The men — the searchers, they have come back! They did not have Granny!" His voice squeaked with excitement.

The Tinker smiled slightly. "Did I not tell you there was no cause to fret?" He bent to examine Tim's toe. "Granny would know just what healing herb to put on, I do not. Go to the spring and wash it. It can do no harm to bind on some of the soft dock that grows near."

Tim hobbled along the pathway, wondering why he must always be in trouble. He had brought disfavor on his family by singing lustily on the Sabbath. He had broken Granny's treasured jar because he had been scared of witches. He had thoughtlessly thrown the fine jackknife away at John's and Ethan's taunting. But even that was not enough. For when he was about to leave he had quarreled with Dorcas, and now he had a sore toe with which to start his journey.

Halfheartedly Tim poured water over his dirt-caked foot. With long, tough grasses, he bound the big dock leaves around his toe. He could not help chuckling a little at his big, green toe.

It was cool here in the deep shade. The earth had a fresh smell after the rain. He lay down on a thick padding of moss, playing hide-and-seek with a sunbeam that tried to find him through the rustling foliage. A wood thrush sang somewhere in a nearby tree, but he felt too lazy to look for it. Among all this loveliness, Tim was still sad. He was going away. Going away — drowsily he closed his eyes.

Half awake, he felt something clutching his shoulder. He tried to wiggle loose and blink his eyes open at the same time. Finally awake, he looked up into his father's face. He sat up then, rubbing his eyes. How long had he slept?

"I have searched everywhere for you. The cart is done, and I need you to help carry while I stow things in the cart-bed. We must get away soon." The Tinker sounded cross.

"I — I did not mean to sleep," Tim stammered.

The Tinker did not reply as he strode toward the cottage. Tim followed as fast as he could.

As his father directed, Tim brought the few simple household articles they would take. A covered basket with clothes, needles and thread, went into a corner. Next a pot and hook, gourd cups, wooden bowls and a dipper. The Tinker put in his tools. Last of all, he laid in his gun, powder horn, and lead.

"Will we meet savage Indians?" Tim could not help asking.

"It is not likely. The dark-skinned brother is friendly enough, if the white man wills to live peaceably, and does not try to take his land unfairly. The war that goes on with the Indian now is far to the west. As for the gun, we will need it to get food, and for protection against wild beasts," his father explained.

The provisions went in next; cornmeal and grits, dried fish and cheese, and a heap of apples and vegetables from the garden which would not keep long in the heat. The whole the Tinker covered with the piece of sailcloth from his shop.

They ate the last of Granny's apple pie and washed it down with milk.

The Tinker barred the door and windows of the cottage. Tim went then to fetch Lucy. He had gone only a few paces toward the wood when he became aware of whispering behind a clump of bushes.

All at once he was not afraid of the whole town. "Come out whoever you are!" The whispering went on. "You are afraid!" Tim challenged.

John stepped out followed by Ethan.

[79]

"You are the coward — running away — afraid of jail!" John taunted.

Ethan shouted, "Coward! Coward!"

An angry flush ran through the freckles on Tim's face. It was the first time he had ever wanted to fight. He lunged at chunky John, swinging his fists.

But firm hands yanked them apart. Tim looked up into his father's face. "It will be easier to be friends some day, if we do nothing to regret

[80]

now," the Tinker said in a slow even voice. Tim dropped his eyes.

John and Ethan stood gaping at them. They dared not talk back to their elders. John nudged Ethan, and looking back over their shoulders, the boys walked away.

When Tim had brought Lucy, he stood at her head in sad silence while his father hitched her to the cart. There would be no time now to make up his quarrel with Dorcas.

6. Vagabonds

W<small>ALKING</small> behind the narrow, loaded cart, tears of frustration rolled down Tim's cheeks. He cared not at all that crying was a childish thing, for he was so miserable about so many things. He had wanted to whale John, and he could have done it, had not his father dragged them apart. He had had no chance to make up his quarrel with Dorcas. There were tasks he would miss, such as driving Daisy to and from pasture, and fetching water from the spring. His toe hurt.

The Tinker, leading Lucy, paid no attention, for the little bay mare was not behaving. Tim did not blame her. She was used to legs on her sides. Her indignation grew at the clumsy bars that made her go in a straight line, and the peculiar thing that kept at her heels as they bumped along the narrow path.

After a while two horsemen rode toward them on the path. Tim's heart thumped as it had when Granny's pursuers had passed their cottage. The Tinker guided Lucy to the edge of the path in a small clearing, to make room for the travelers.

The man on the big brown horse reined up beside them. "It is rare to find a cart on the country road. You are quite enterprising, my good man. What is your trade?"

Tim's father drew up to his full height. "I am a tinker, sir," he said.

The other man nodded his approval. "It is time the people of this land traveled on wheels. When more do so, the authorities will take the trouble to make the roads fit for travel."

[83]

After another curious look at the cart, the men spurred their horses and were away. Tim drew a breath of relief. "Who are they, Father?"

"Doubtless they are merchants of Boston on business to Salem," the Tinker replied, quieting Tim's fears.

When Tim's feet lagged, his father bade him ride on the cart. So, riding and walking, the afternoon went by. At sundown, they came to a wayside trough, hollowed from a huge log and filled constantly with cool water from a spring.

"It is a good place to spend the night," said the Tinker, unhitching Lucy from the cart.

Tim stood by Lucy while she drank deeply, then he turned her out to graze. The Tinker and Tim busied themselves with victuals. The place had probably been an Indian camp, for campfires had been kindled here and there. When Tim had gathered dry wood, his father struck a fire, Indian fashion, with a flint. The pot of vegetables he had washed and cut with his jackknife were soon bubbling merrily where they hung from a sapling lug pole, set across two forked sticks.

They made their bed that night under the trees. Though Tim missed the comfort of his attic feather bed, he slept soundly.

In the gray of dawn, they were on their way again. The first pink glow of sunrise was coloring the sky when Tim heard a cock crow. Where cocks were, people lived. A short distance ahead they came upon a little farmhouse, nestled among trees at the edge of a large clearing.

"Yo-ho!" the Tinker hailed lustily, leading Lucy toward the cottage.

A tall string bean of a man came from a rail-fenced enclosure behind the house, carrying a wooden pail of milk. A woman, as squat and round as her husband was lanky, came to the door, three small children peeking from behind her skirts.

"Well, well! The Tinker!" Farmer Tate exclaimed heartily. "The little Tinker, too! Just in time to eat."

"Is your haystack soft this summer?" inquired Tim's father, quirking an eyebrow at the farmer.

"Soft as goose down," the farmer laughed, slapping his leather breeches leg. "But there is much to be done before haystack time."

The woman giggled. "The house would go to ruin, Tinker, if you did not come. That husband of mine will never lift a hand to mend." Farmer Tate chuckled at their family joke. "You are coming up in the world, with such a fine cart," the woman said admiringly. Tim liked them at once.

After a hearty breakfast of porridge and fresh milk, together with the salt fish the Tinker brought from the cart, Tim lost some of his shyness. All day, while his father mended, he trotted at Farmer Tate's heels.

At the end of the busy day, when the sun had rolled down behind the woods in flaming splendor, the Tinker sang his rollicking songs. Tim and the farmer joined in; Tim with his piping treble, and Farmer Tate in his rumbling bass. There was talk, too, of witchcraft doings in Salem, for the farmer and his wife were eager for news. But Tim grew sleepy.

Presently, then, the Tetlows were cozy in the fragrant haystack. Tim watched the stars above.

The same stars were shining on Granny, and on Salem where Daisy and the Whitcombs were, he thought drowsily.

The Tates lived a free and happy life and Tim was sorry when, two days later, he and his father hitched Lucy to the cart and moved on. So was Lucy. Again she did not behave well until she was convinced that those wooden bars along her sides were there to stay.

That afternoon they approached a village at the seaside. Tim knew that it must be Lynn, for the Tinker had told him that they would go there. They stopped by the wayside while Tim picked a thorn from his bare, calloused foot. Wondering what might lie ahead of them, he scratched the itching spot on his healing toe. He liked the open country best, for there ugly thoughts of witches seemed far away.

Tim's father stooped to examine his son's travel-worn feet. "In Lynn there is a shoemaker who makes the finest shoes in the colonies. Perhaps he will make you a pair of Indian moccasins to protect your feet from the rough way, lad."

[87]

"But, Father, you have no money to buy moccasins," Tim said gravely. "And my Sabbath shoes must be saved for churchgoing."

"The shoemaker is my friend," the Tinker said simply.

When they came into Lynn, the Tinker drove Lucy at once to the cobbler's shop, and tied her to a post in front. Inside the shop, the shoemaker looked up from his pegging, a warm smile spreading over his rugged, red face.

"If it is not the Tinker of Salem! It is long since I have set eyes on you, my friend," he said heartily.

While the old friends talked Tim walked about the shop. He stared with amazement at the shelves of fine shoes. The boots for men bore carved silver buckles, such as no Puritan would ever wear. Those for fine dames were tiny, high of heel, and of softest leather or fabric. The ladies who danced at great balls, as Dorcas said, must wear these dainty slippers.

It was the shoemaker himself who noticed Tim's bare, sore feet. He made a peculiar clicking noise with his tongue against his teeth, while he shook his head. "Come here, lad, and try these on for size." He took a pair of soft, but stout, moccasins from beneath a shelf and held them out to Tim.

Tim's blue eyes shone as he slipped them on. He wiggled his toes to feel the comfort of them. "No one will buy the Indian shoes now, yet no foot covering is so easy for treading the wilderness paths."

Shyness took hold of Tim, and he could say nothing.

"The lad means well, for I know the thankfulness in his heart," the Tinker made excuse for him.

"That I know," the cobbler agreed.

Tim found the use of his tongue then. "Is there not some task I can do?"

The shoemaker pulled his lower lip. "Perhaps — come tomorrow."

When they left the cobbler shop, Tim asked, "Where will we lodge in the village, Father?"

"We will go to The Anchor. There is always tinkering to be done about the tavern, and there will be shelter for us somewhere," the Tinker said.

When they reached the tavern, they found the white-haired landlord busy greeting two distinguished-looking men who had just dismounted from their horses. "Welcome to The Anchor! The best fare of my tavern is at the disposal of the magistrates of the law." He saluted stiffly in soldier fashion, for he had been one of Oliver Cromwell's soldiers in England and had fled to the colonies when England again came under the rule of a king and queen.

The Tinker hastily led Lucy around to the back of the inn. Tim followed closely, feeling uneasy, though he knew not why. He forgot the feeling as he watched the games of quoits and shuffleboard going on in the innyard. So interested was he that he was not much help unharnessing Lucy. While he tied her in the horse shelter, he watched the play over his shoulder.

Then the landlord came hurriedly from the kitchen door, rubbing his hands together in an excited way. He cleared his throat. "Gentlemen, the Puritan magistrates have arrived. They regard gaming with disfavor — sports will have to stop for the present."

With much grumbling, the guests left their games and went back into the tavern. The landlord, with the help of the boy who had brought the magistrates' horses to the shelter, gathered up the rings and staffs, and the boy carried them away. It was only then that the innkeeper noticed Tim and his father.

A big smile spread over his pleasant face. "If it isn't the Tinker — and with a cart! This your lad?" and he rumpled Tim's bright hair. "You are most welcome, Tinker Tetlow, for there is much about the tavern in need of fixing." He chattered on, asking Tim's father questions, but giving him no time to reply.

Tim kept close to his father as he tinkered on furniture and broken shutters, in the washhouse at the back of the tavern. Once, when he had ventured to the front of the inn, he had heard the Puritan magistrates talking of witches and trials and hangings, and his heart had beat hard. The men were on their way to Salem to help in the trials, his father said. Tim thought of Granny, and remembering the warning of the searchers, he was not at all sure that his father was safe.

The next morning the Tinker set about mending broken chairs. Tim felt lonely and of no use.

"Father, would it not be well if I went to the cobbler shop?" he asked. "Maybe there is an errand I can run to earn my moccasins."

His father nodded absently, fitting a leg to a chair. "Do not be gone long, lad."

When Tim entered the shop the shoemaker emptied his mouth of pegs and smiled. "Two pair of plain boots, a Puritan magistrate of Boston ordered made, when he was last here. I hear he is now at The Anchor. Will you take them to him, Tim? He is the big man with the wart on his cheek."

Tim could feel his heart beating hard again. Could he walk up to the big, stern Puritan — even to show his gratitude for his new moccasins? He watched his toes pushing the soft leather up and down.

The shoemaker frowned in a puzzled way.

"If I have set you too hard a task — " he began.

"Oh, no-o, sir," Tim stammered, swallowing the scared feeling in his throat.

The cobbler pulled two pairs of big boots from a low shelf. "Don't forget, it is the man with the wart and the black hair. I have the price of the boots."

When Tim reached the inn, the boots under his arm, his knees were trembling, and sweat wet the palms of his hands. The boy was struck dumb as the big Puritan stepped from the door just as he reached it. Without a word, he held the boots toward the man.

"If they are not my new boots! Are you the shoemaker's son?" the man said, taking the boots.

"No-o, sir. I am but a traveler," Tim managed to reply.

"A traveler — and so young? Mind you do not fall into evil ways," the man admonished.

"No — yes, sir." Tim was not sure of anything, for his mind was in a frightened whirl.

"Here is twopence for you, my lad, and God's

blessing on you." The pompous man pressed the money into Tim's damp hand.

Tim ran to the washroom without a word. Here he poured out his tale to his father, who quieted his fears. Later, when he overheard the Tinker and the cobbler chuckling over the matter, he knew his fright had been for nothing.

The day came when everything at the tavern was in fine order, and Tim and his father went on their way again. Both hard and happy times came to them as they journeyed, going only short distances each day, but most of the time they were happy. They seldom hung their pot over a camp-fire, for everywhere the Tinker was welcome. Berries were ripe on the hillsides, and the purple smear on Tim's face and the snagged places in his breeches told of their goodness.

"Sing, Father!" Tim cried lightheartedly.

He joined in joyously. A bird eyed them from a wayside tree, then flew ahead to another tree. Tim laughed at it.

"The bird likes it, for he winked at me," Tim declared with an impish grin.

"Such fancy! No doubt you will see witches riding again." Tim's father flicked the flies from Lucy's back, a carefree twinkle in his eye.

Sometimes they had to be helped from bogs, when the little bay mare floundered in the mire and the wheels sank to the hub. Usually there was a farmhouse not too far distant, to which Tim would run for help from neighborly country people. Now, too, there were more streams to be forded. When they left Malden and came toward Medford, Tim looked with dismay at the river they must cross. Many times Lucy had pulled the cart after her across streams, but this one was wide and deep.

"How will we get across, Father?" Tim's face was anxious.

The Tinker stood, pulling his ear, before he replied. "Never before have I had a cart to contend with. Always before I have found someone to row me across in a boat, while Lucy swam."

Just then a villager came up grinning. "Your newfangled contraption a bit hard to get across the river, eh?"

[95]

The Tinker grinned back at him. "I am pondering ways and means," he admitted.

This pleased the man. "I have a prime Indian dugout. We can use it, if you've a mind to — and can figure out ways and means," he chuckled.

After much discussion they formed a plan. They took the cart apart. Piece by piece they took it across the river in the canoe. When the wheels and bed were over, their new-found friend rowed Tim and the axletree over, while Lucy swam along behind.

When the cart was again assembled, the man looked at it with his head on one side. "Not such a bad contraption! Some day, doubtless, there'll be many like it in the country."

And they were on their way again. Since Lucy had learned the ways of a cart horse, they both rode at once, Tim with his feet hanging over the back of the cart. On they went until they came in sight of Charlestown on a late July morning.

"What is Charlestown like?" Tim wanted to know.

"Much like Salem, lad. There are fisheries and

merchant houses, and the ships come in from the sea," said his father.

"Oh!" Tim frowned, stooping to rub a scuffed spot on his moccasins. "Must we go there?"

"There are friends there, who will gladly give me work," and his father clucked to Lucy.

Tim looked at his father uneasily. "If it is like Salem — do people there believe in witches?"

"Perhaps some do. Withal, it is a friendly place and peaceful."

They had come through Charlestown Neck and down the hill into the town. Soon they stopped before a large house with many gables, set back in a blooming flower garden. They drove to the side of the house, where Tim tied Lucy to the hitching post, with the slip loop his father had taught him. Then he followed the Tinker to the open kitchen door, standing close while his father tapped on the doorframe.

7. The Jar Like Granny's

A BUSTLING woman, in a plain dress and kerchief, with smooth dark hair tucked under a white cap, was mixing dough. "Come in," she called cheerily. Then she looked at them over her plump shoulder. "If it isn't the Tinker! You are as welcome as July rain! For months our chairs have needed mending. My husband grows as big as a house, doing nothing but sit. Dame Clive's chairs crumple under Ebenezer as though they were made of bark. And he is no good at fixing things at all."

The Tinker chuckled. "The garden is as neat as your black hair, Hannah. If Ebenezer does nothing but sit, who weeds the beds and loosens the soil, do you?"

"Now —" flustered Hannah began. Tim did not mean to snicker, but the little laugh came right out. The woman, noticing him for the first time, smiled broadly. "Is this your lad, Tinker? He looks to be fine and hearty. The traveling about will do him good, all but that pretty red hair of his. The sun is bleaching it."

Tim blushed. Stepping bashfully behind his father, he hung his head.

"He is a likely lad." Tim's heart thumped at the pride in his father's voice.

"What of the witches in Salem? It is little news we hear. It is said the Boston jail is filled with Salem witches. Why there should be so many more witches in Salem than elsewhere is beyond my thinking," Hannah chattered.

The Tinker said earnestly, "They are not witches, Hannah, but honest and kindly people, falsely accused by those who bear a grudge."

[100]

Hannah clicked her tongue. "For shame!" she said.

When his elders were absorbed in talk, Tim tiptoed around the room. In a big cupboard, standing beside the huge fireplace, were the finest dishes he had ever seen. Some were of polished pewter; some were of sparkling glass. There were gaily decorated pieces of crockery and china. As Tim followed the orderly rows with his eyes, his breath suddenly stopped. He stepped closer to peer at a stoneware jar with a pewter lid. It was the same as Granny's — or was it? He reached out to trace the design with a finger, as he had often done with Granny's.

"Tim!" His father's voice was unnaturally sharp. The boy jumped guiltily and hung his head. "Did you not learn from Granny not to meddle?"

Tim nodded miserably. He had disgraced his father. The Tinker had not noticed the jar, but of what use was it to tell him about it?

Hannah looked from the boy to his father. "The lad meant no harm. Dame Clive's dishes are well worth gazing at."

[101]

Tim frowned at his feet, wishing he were away somewhere else. Then a great shadow fell across the floor, and he looked up shyly at a tall, bulky man, standing in the doorway, swabbing the sweat from his face.

"Glad you are here, Tinker Tetlow," Ebenezer rumbled. "Chairs are flimsy. No wonder they fall to pieces under me." His deep laugh warmed Tim's heart.

"What you need, Ebenezer, is a good stout chair, on which you could sit and laugh to your heart's content. I could build such a chair," the Tinker said shrewdly.

"And well it would pay Dame Clive to have it built," Hannah agreed.

Ebenezer laughed again, and Tim went a little closer to see his big frame shake. Suddenly he stopped laughing. He widened his eyes at Tim in a comical fashion. "What have we here, a young tinker?" He reached out and roughed Tim's bright hair. Tim grinned up at him. "On second thought, you would make a fine gardener's helper."

[102]

In his eagerness, Tim forgot his bashfulness. "I helped in the garden at home."

Ebenezer drew his heavy brows together. "Know a carrot from a wild parsnip?" he teased.

Before Tim could tell him that he knew weeds and vegetables apart, the most beautiful woman he had ever seen came into the room. Her curls were not covered by a cap; her shell-pink cheeks were dimpled, and her silken skirts rustled as she walked. She was a hollyhock doll sort of person, Tim thought. He wished that Dorcas could see her.

She smiled as she said, "I am glad you have come, Tinker Tetlow. No one mends as you do."

"I thank you for your kindness," the Tinker said, bowing.

"Hannah, be sure that everything is made as good as new before he leaves," the beautiful lady directed.

"Yes, Dame Clive. And he says he can make a chair stout enough to hold Ebenezer up!" Hannah folded her hands and puckered her lips.

Dame Clive's laughter rippled like a brook. "By all means have him build it." It was then that she noticed Tim. "What is your name, lad?"

"I am Tim, the Tinker's son."

"A well-favored lad. You must be proud of him," she smiled at Tim's father. "Be sure you give him plenty of victuals, Hannah."

Tim's eyes followed her as she swished through the doorway into the other part of the big house. Dainty shoes, such as Tim had seen on the shelves of the Lynn cobbler shop, peeked from below her skirts.

Out at the hitching post, Lucy was pawing impatiently. Ebenezer, looking out the door, saw her. "Come, Tim, we will unhitch the little mare and turn her into the pasture with the big grays." Tim followed him to the coach house, leading Lucy. Ebenezer stood off to admire the Tinker's cart. Then he laughed heartily. "I doubt not that the Tinker can build me a stout chair, now that I have seen his new cart. We will find a place for it in the coach house."

When the coach house doors were opened, Tim

looked, goggle-eyed, at the fine coach inside. "Oh!" he breathed.

Ebenezer grinned. "Dame Clive must needs have an English coach, in which to ride about the town. And even over to Boston she goes, though the vehicle will not go on the ferry boats without a taking apart and a putting together again!" The big man shook his head over the vanity of his mistress.

Tim said, "We had to take our cart apart to cross the river, a while back."

Leading Lucy, Tim followed Ebenezer down the path to the pasture behind the coach house. Two big gray horses lifted their heads and neighed when they saw Lucy. When he slipped the bridle from the mare's head, Tim whispered in her ear, "Lucy, I have found a jar like Granny's — but I can never possess it." The little bay rubbed her nose against him, and he liked to think she understood his trouble. But she cantered away, kicking up her heels before the big gray beauties.

Ebenezer took him to the garden and set him to weeding beans. In the kitchen garden were herbs and vegetables of all kinds. The big flower garden was elegant. There grew the biggest hollyhocks he had ever seen. Again he thought of Dorcas.

Tim worked industriously. It was hot, and the sky was soon covered with scurrying gray clouds. Big drops of rain began to pelt him.

"Come, Tim, there is no need to stay in the rain. Weeds will pull easier after the soil is wet." Ebenezer puffed toward the kitchen with Tim at his heels.

Hannah was carrying glass and china dishes from the dining room, and stacking them neatly on the kitchen table. She had served Dame Clive and her husband. Now she put dinner for the Tinker and Tim, Ebenezer and herself, on a table in the center of the kitchen. Tim stood, as was manners to do, even after Ebenezer had asked the blessing, until Ebenezer invited him to sit with them. Granny always let him sit, unless there were guests.

His back was to the crockery jar. But he thought of it all the while he ate Hannah's good cooking.

When the meal ended, the rain still came down. Tim sidled over to the cupboard, his hands clasped tightly behind him. Now, he was sure the jar was like Granny's.

Hannah cleared the table with a clatter. "When I have finished with the glass and china, I could use a good hand with the pewter drying, lad."

Tim had often helped Granny and was glad to help Hannah now. Whenever he carried a dish to the cupboard he paused to look, until Hannah asked curiously, "Whatever are you looking at?"

Tim turned red in confusion. "The — the pretty jar — it is like the one Granny had," he stammered.

"You mean the clumsy, crockery one? Dame Clive never uses it since she has the fine ones of glass and china," Hannah told him.

"I broke Granny's, the night I got scared of witches," Tim confessed. "She prized it highly, for her mother had brought it from England."

Hannah opened her eyes wide. "Witches? Tell me about them." She bobbed her head as Tim told her of the sight he had seen on the wilderness trail, of his foolish fears and of all that had happened that night, after he had broken Granny's precious jar. "What a shame," Hannah said sympathetically.

That night as they settled down to sleep in the coach house loft, Tim told his father of the jar like Granny's. But the Tinker said firmly, "Think no more of it, lad. It is wrong to covet."

After that Tim tried not to want it. But he could not stop his heart from yearning after it.

Tim thought often of Salem, and of the friends there who had turned against him. Though he had no young companions here in Charlestown, he was content to be with Ebenezer, helping in the garden and with the big gray horses. When free from tasks, he sometimes rode Lucy around the pasture, followed by the big grays.

One day he helped Ebenezer harness the handsome team to the coach, for Dame Clive was of a mind to go shopping. Tim stood back when the Hollyhock Lady — he would always think of her as the Hollyhock Lady — came out to the coach.

"My husband is going today to help me choose

in the shops. Two ships have come in loaded with choice goods. Ebenezer, your services will not be needed." Then she spied Tim, standing apart. "Tim, come here!" She smiled at him. "How would you like to ride along and watch the grays, while we are in the shops?" Tim looked at his bare feet, too bashful to reply. The Hollyhock Lady laughed her tinkling laugh. "You are quite proper. Jump up on the back of the coach."

When Richard Clive came from the house, Tim could not help gaping at his coat of finest fabric all trimmed with buttons and gold lace. The merchant lowered the step and helped his wife to a seat in the coach.

Perched on the back, Tim saw people stare at them from the doorways where they had fled out of the path of the spirited team. Dogs barked indignantly at the passing coach.

When they came to the shops, Tim jumped down and tied the grays to a post. He stood by, keeping watch over them.

"You must be from the back country," said a voice.

Tim jumped. A boy, finely clad, stood regarding Tim curiously. Tim knew from the cut of his lined breeches, silver-buttoned waistcoat, topped by a lace cravat, that his folks were wealthy.

"I am not from the back country. I come from Salem," Tim said, frowning.

"There are witches there," the boy stated flatly.

"No!" Tim denied. "Witches are not real."

"So! The jail in Boston is crammed with witches brought from Salem," the boy contradicted.

Tim said quickly, "They are falsely accused. Just as Granny had to flee —" he stopped then, biting his lip.

"Your grandmother must be a witch then!" his tormentor cried.

"It is not true!" Tim said vehemently.

"Ah-ha! If she is here she will surely be put in Boston jail."

Tim was glad that the Clives came from the shop then, and they went on their way. The old fears were coming back to him, and he wished to leave the town.

That night in the hayloft he said, "Father, when will we leave Charlestown?"

"I thought you were well content here, Tim." Tim told his father then of what the boy on the street had said that day. "Lad, everywhere there will be some who are so minded. But have no fears, for we are in no danger, and Granny is long since safe."

One day Hannah said to Tim, "Come here, lad." She turned him about, clicking her tongue. "Doubtless the berries you had by the wayside tasted good, but the briars have snagged your breeches until you are scarcely decent." She fetched an old pair of deerskin breeches, belonging to Ebenezer, and held them up, smiling. "Enough whole skin left for your size," she nodded.

Tim stood still while Hannah measured and cut. When she was absorbed in stitching the soft leather, Tim tiptoed over for another look at the jar.

Then on the Sabbath Tim put on his Sabbath shoes and the new breeches Hannah had made for him. He and the Tinker walked with Hannah and

Ebenezer to the meetinghouse, which Tim found to be much like the one in Salem, even in its strictness.

That week when Tim told Ebenezer about Dorcas and her hollyhock dolls, and about the quarrel they had, the kind gardener gave him seed of the biggest hollyhock plant. Tim wrapped the seed in a dock leaf and carried it to their hamper.

The Tinker had finally mended everything about the place. He had finished Ebenezer's stout chair, which the big man declared fitted him exactly, even to his laugh. Now they must go. His fears stilled again, Tim was sorry to leave.

Much to her disgust, Lucy was hitched to the cart. She did not like leaving the handsome gray horses and the tender grass of the meadow. Ebenezer loaded the cart with hay, saying, "You will not need to stop for grazing this day." Hannah brought a lunch wrapped in a cloth.

But Tim could not go without one more fond look at the jar like Granny's. He ran to the kitchen, where he stood motionless before the cupboard. He wished so hard that he did not hear

light footsteps until they were beside him. He raised startled blue eyes to the face of the Hollyhock Lady. He had not touched it. But what would she think? He began to tremble and his heart seemed to go to the soles of his moccasined feet, weighing him to the floor.

"What is it, Tim?" the lovely lady asked lightly.

Tim struggled to make his tongue move. "The jar — like Granny's I broke. I only — wanted to look — at it again," he murmured jerkily.

[113]

"This one?" Dame Clive touched the pewter lid, looking at him questioningly. Tim nodded wordlessly. She took the jar from the shelf and put it in his shaking hands.

"I — I did not mean — I only meant to look," Tim floundered. Only his shining eyes could speak his gratitude.

"Do not say a word, lad, for you have earned it. Ebenezer has told me how willingly you helped him. And Hannah says she does not know what she will do without you," Dame Clive said.

Scarcely breathing, Tim carried his treasure to the cart on feet as light as goose down. But what would his father say?

8. Adventures on the Way

Tɪᴍ's heart was beating furiously as he came to the cart. He held the jar tight in his hands.

The Tinker regarded him gravely. "You did not ask for it?" he questioned sternly.

"No, Father, I did not. And Dame Clive says I earned it." Tim's eyes held a mixture of pride and anxiety, lest his father would not let him keep the jar like Granny's.

"That he did," Ebenezer agreed heartily. "Do

not scold the lad for wanting to please his grand-mother, Tinker."

That settled the matter. Hannah bustled about, packing the crockery jar in an empty space in the hamper. Tim climbed on the cart, and Ebenezer brought a handful of apples as a parting gift. Calling good-by to the people in the big house, they were vagabonds again.

As they left the town behind, going westward, the Tinker said, "When we come to Cambridge, we will take the Old Connecticut Path for a while. Not often have I been this far in my tinkering, but some day perhaps, the Divine Providence willing, you will have a great surprise." And he chuckled under his breath.

"Will I see Granny?" Tim asked eagerly.

Tim's father grinned lightheartedly. "A surprise is not a surprise if it be told."

Although Tim knew that teasing never gained him anything, still he began to tease. His father only started a song of the sea, and Tim could do nothing but join in.

It was near noon when they came to a stretch of

deep woods beyond Cambridge. They were about to stop for a noontime rest, when they heard the beat of horses' hoofs on the soft path around the bend behind them. Tim pulled Lucy to one side and stopped. A big black horse, bearing a man and a woman, swung around the curve. Tim saw at once that it was Quaker Heath with a good woman of the Salem church. Their friend reined up beside them.

"They come fast after us!" Quaker Heath, like his big mount, was breathing heavily. "I could not take the wilderness road, as I did with Granny Tetlow, for I was not sure the friendly Indian would be at the appointed place to guide us through."

"It does my heart good to see that they have not jailed you for aiding witches," the Tinker said warmly.

"As yet, they have no evidence that I have anything to do with the escape of witchcraft victims." The Quaker mopped his face. "They cannot be far behind now. Perhaps thee can aid us."

"We will take care of Ellen Ross," said the Tinker.

Quaker Heath dismounted and helped the woman to the ground, and Tim's father pulled the hay aside and told her to curl up in the bottom of the cart. He spread hay over her lightly.

"I'll unbridle Lucy," said Tim, as his father carried the leftover hay and piled it under the little mare's greedy nose.

"Thee is a quick-witted man, and a kind one." The big Quaker patted his horse's quivering neck.

"We have had kindness at your hands, too," said the Tinker. "Now you must get to safety. There is a narrow path, almost hidden by brush, a few paces back. Go take it and stay in the woods until your pursuers have gone."

Tim stood tense and still until he saw the flanks of the black horse disappear in the underbrush, and he could no longer hear the crackling of twigs. His heartbeats tried to stop his breath.

"We must appear to be nooning," said the Tinker, taking Hannah's food from the hamper he had set out of the cart.

[118]

When they heard the horsemen coming, Tim was stuffing a piece of Hannah's delicious huckleberry pie down his unwilling throat. The Tinker leaned against a wheel munching, with apparent enjoyment, another hunk of the luscious pie.

"Quiet — they come," he warned the heap of hay in the cart.

When the horses drew up beside them, Tim saw with relief that the men were not the same as those who had searched their cottage for Granny.

A swarthy man looked down at Tim's father. "Well, well! If it is not Tinker Tetlow of Salem. What, I pray, are you doing away down here?"

The Tinker drew himself up and said with dignity, "I am earning my bread among kind friends. The village of Salem denied me that."

"Hoity-toity!" the man exclaimed. "Getting high and mighty all at once!"

A scrawny man fixed piercing eyes on Tim's father. "Did you see a horseman go by with a witch behind?"

"What kind of a horseman?" drawled the

Tinker, taking another bite of pie. The man watched him hungrily.

"That we have never been close enough to see," the man grumbled. "In the towns we have come through, people have seen them but they do not agree. Some say the man was big and well-favored, riding a big brown horse; but others say he was an ugly, broad man on a black. In Cambridge, they say a horseman, with a woman on a pillion behind, came this way, but we cannot tell." The man rubbed a weary hand across his forehead.

The Tinker took another bite of pie, and the rich, purple juice ran. "No horseman has passed us this day, has he, Tim?" Tim shook his head, for it was true.

The third man said impatiently, "He is telling the truth, for I never knew the Tinker to lie. They have gone another way. What does it matter? The witch is out of our midst."

"We are foolish to wear out our good horses to bring witches to trial, when our jail is bulging now," said the scrawny man.

Then the men turned their lathered horses,

and went slowly back around the bend out of sight. When all sound of them had died away, the Tinker pulled the hay from Ellen Ross. She sat up, brushing the hay from her cap.

"I am ever so grateful to you, Tinker Tetlow," she said.

"Why did they call you a witch?" Tim asked.

The woman sighed deeply. "I spoke openly against the falsehoods foolish people were shrieking about all the good people now shut in jail. Then, since I could not agree, they began to cry out that I, too, was a witch. They were coming to take me, when Quaker Heath rescued me. I never want to see Salem again," Ellen Ross said bitterly.

"Oh, come now! Eat a bite with us. Hannah's excellent cooking will change your way of looking at things." The Tinker gave her dried fish, corn-cake and pie. "Where are you bound for?"

"My sister lives in a farm village a little farther on. She will take me in." Ellen Ross began to eat hungrily.

"We will take you to your folks, for we are bound for Worcester," the Tinker told her.

Tim bounced off the cart. "That is where Aunt Susie lives! Is Granny there? Will I see Cousin Seth, and Cousin Polly, and the little cousins?"

"Sooner or later, maybe." His father grinned provokingly.

"Susie Tetlow she was, before she married Ezra Williams, the miller of Worcester," said Ellen Ross. "Well I remember how we played together when we were little." Her face lit up as she talked of pleasant things. Tim thought her pretty, with her dark hair, and the pink that had come back into her cheeks.

As they journeyed along, through valleys and over hills, they talked of Salem doings. Few of the unfortunate people accused of witchcraft had been able to flee, Ellen Ross told them. Some of those who had taken passage by water to other cities had been caught and returned, to be put in jail. The country people of the land were not so worried about witchcraft, and so the backwoods farms and villages made a safe refuge for some of the accused.

It was sundown when they came to the farm home of Ellen Ross's sister. They found a welcome there, with a sweet-smelling haystack for a bed, and fresh milk to drink. It made Tim think again of Daisy, and wonder how she liked being cared for by the Whitcombs. Then he looked in their basket to make sure the seeds of the biggest holly-hock were safe.

They were in a friendly neighborhood, with work to be done in the village. And so it was at other places as they ambled along. The Tinker exchanged his clever work for shelter and food, and an occasional coin. Everywhere people were eager for news, and always they liked his songs.

Along the lonely stretches of road they lived on wild game, grits, and the wild berries that grew by the wayside. Once they saw a black panther, crouching in the dense forest. The Tinker had his gun ready to fire when the beast slunk away, much to Tim's relief. The howling of wolves in the night had ceased to frighten Tim.

They reached Marlborough and turned south-ward toward Worcester on the Old Bay Path. When it rained, they were thankful for the sun-shine that followed afterward to dry their clothing. There were streams to ford, and hills to go up and down.

"Here are fine willows for whistles," the Tinker said.

Tim gathered the willow rods and made the whistles as they went along. He soon learned to loosen the bark, trim and notch the wood, then slip the bark back in place. Each whistle had a different note, so Tom filled his pocket with them for his cousins.

At last they came to Worcester and inquired the way to Miller Williams's house. Tim's eyes were wide with expectation, his heart beat high, wondering if his surprise would be a sight of Granny.

As they drew up beside the gabled house, a pink-cheeked woman came to the door. She ran out to meet the Tinker and kissed him soundly on both cheeks.

"I knew you would come, brother! And this is Tim." The boy pulled away bashfully as she kissed him, too.

Cousins came spilling from the doorway. The

[124]

lanky boy, about Tim's age, must be Seth. The girl with the bright hair and the big, blue eyes was surely Polly. Two small children hung back shyly.

The whir of the spinning wheel inside the house stopped. Granny's small figure appeared in the doorway. Tim ran to her crying, "Granny! Granny!" She folded him into her arms.

"Have you been a good lad?" she asked, kissing him, which he did not mind at all.

"I have tried, Granny." Remembering the stone jar, he lugged the hamper from the cart, and pulled out the jar. "See, Granny, I earned it for you myself when we were in Charlestown."

Granny took the jar and looked at it wonderingly. "It is just like my own old jar. This one I will prize even more highly, because you earned it for me."

The cousins crowded around. Tim found Seth standing at his elbow. Thrusting his hands deep into the pockets of his deerskin breeches, he pulled out the whistles. The longest he offered to Seth.

His cousin blew a loud note on it. "Never heard

a louder one," Seth gave his opinion, holding it toward Tim.

"It is yours," said Tim.

Seth grinned his thanks and stepped along, blowing loudly. Polly drew shyly near, and Tim gave her one, too. In another moment they had formed a merry brigade, marching along to the piping of the willow whistles. The younger cousins, except the baby in the cradle, fell in behind. The big white geese honked indignantly at them for making so much noise.

The older folks looked on and laughed. This, Tim thought, would be a jolly place to live.

"Pipe for me while I dance my cornhusk dolls," Polly coaxed, when they were tired of marching.

That reminded Tim of the big hollyhock seed. He ran to the house and lifted the withered dock leaf from the hamper. In the yard he told them about Dorcas and her hollyhock dolls, about the tithing man, and about his promise to bring Dorcas the biggest hollyhock seed he could find. He told them how he and Dorcas had quarreled,

[127]

and that he had found the seed at Charlestown to take her as a peace offering.

"What does Dorcas look like?" Polly asked curiously.

Tim moved his hands to show how tall she came to him, and how her curls were always creeping from her cap. Suddenly the dry leaf split, scattering the seeds upon the ground. Before the children could gather them up, the geese closed in on them, scooping them up with their bills.

"Oh," Tim moaned, "I will have no peace gift for Dorcas!"

"Our hollyhocks have seed," Polly tried to console him. "Come see."

Tim eyed the bent and seeded stocks with disdain. "They are no bigger than the Whitcombs'."

In the big, pleasant Williams house there was room for them all. Uncle Ezra, the miller, was well thought of, and could provide bountifully for his family. When the Tinker was not busy mending, there was work at the mill for him.

As for Lucy, if it had not been for the many rides the children took, the little mare would have grown fat and lazy. She grazed daily with the two Williams' cows in the meadow.

There were no wharves, where they could watch the fishing boats come in. But there was a creek, where Tim and Seth and other Worcester boys swam, or fished for shiners in the clear pools.

Tasks aplenty there were, too. Tim helped Seth weed the garden and corn patch. He helped him round up the pigs when they escaped from their sty. The flock of geese was always wandering off, to be driven home again.

Sometimes at twilight, Tim told Seth and Polly about the happenings in Salem. Polly would shudder, then giggle at the thought of witches.

As the late summer days crept by, Granny, too, was always busy. One day Tim stood watching her run tallow into the candle molds and hang them to set.

"Mother, I do not know what I will do without you, when it comes time for you to go back to Salem," her daughter said.

Granny smiled. "You managed very well, Susanna, before I came."

Tim bent toward his grandmother earnestly. "Granny, could we not go on living here always?"

Granny shook her head. "Would you want never to go back to Salem to live?"

"It is friendly here," Tim declared.

Granny looked into the distance dreamily. "We have good friends in Salem. I keep wondering how the Whitcomb baby is getting along, and how Betsy is managing everything."

"They have Daisy's milk and our vegetable patch," Tim reminded her.

Granny sighed. "Yes. But Betsy is too young to know what to do if sickness comes. She knows nothing of herbs and how to brew them." An anxious pucker came into her face.

Another kind of pucker came into Tim's face. Aunt Susie saw it and laughed. "Your Granny's herb tea may not taste very good, Tim, but you would not be here today had she not known what to give you for chills and fever."

"Our home is Salem." Granny hung a candle mold with a decided little click. Tim knew they would be going back.

When September came, the leaves began turning bright, and the wild geese, calling overhead, flew south. With October, the leaves began to tumble from the trees, and the air grew chill. The mill wheel turned from dawn to dark, for farmers were bringing their corn to the mill to be ground into grit and meal for the winter. The Tinker worked with Uncle Ezra these days. And before they knew it, cold November days were upon them.

One day when Tim and Seth were penning up the pigs, they looked up to see the Tinker come running down the road. At some distance he began waving his arms and shouting. The squeals of the pigs drowned out his words. Tim and Seth left the pigs to stray and ran toward the house.

From the house came Granny, Aunt Susie, and Polly. And there they all stood, shivering and waiting for they knew not what.

9. Back to Salem

TIM, Granny, and the Williams family crowded around the Tinker. "I talked with Henry Pryor, who just came from Boston. He says that Governor Phips has issued a reprieve to all under sentence of death for witchcraft, and that there will be no more hangings. A pretty pass affairs had come to, when even the governor's wife was accused. The governor has sent a letter to King William and Queen Mary about the unjust trials."

Breathlessly, Tim's father looked from one pleased face to another, smiling broadly.

"Thanks be to the Divine Providence," Granny said reverently. "People have come to their senses and we can go home to Salem."

"We will miss you all, but Mother's heart is set on going back. The icy winter is almost upon us; if you must go, it is well that you go at once," Aunt Susie said briskly.

Tim felt half glad, half sad. He wanted to see the Whitcombs. He wondered if John and Ethan would be friends again. Yet, he was reluctant to leave the Williams household.

That day the womenfolk set about preparing food for the journey, for the Tetlows would not stop for much tinkering on the way. Early the next morning they set out, shouting good-bys. Promises to visit each other another day flew back and forth.

Sometimes Granny rode in the bumpy cart; sometimes she walked. Tim walked or rode Lucy, for he had found it easier than the jolts of the cart. The Tinker was always afoot.

When evening came, they found a welcome at some farm fireside, where they would sing or tell stories of Salem. For Granny there was always a bed inside, but many nights Tim and the Tinker burrowed deep into the sheltered side of a haystack.

Often Granny would teach the farmer's wife some new weaving stitch, or a new way to cook corn. Though they did not tarry long, there was sometimes a bit of mending the Tinker could do, and he would feel better for earning his food.

There were days when the cold winds tore at the warm capes Granny had spun and woven and sewed for them during the summer. But all together the journey eastward did not seem as long as the westward journey had been. Having Granny along was such a comfort to Tim.

"Will we stop in Charlestown, Father?" Tim asked, for he knew it would lengthen their journey to go there.

"Yes. Ebenezer and Hannah will be watching for us." Then the Tinker chuckled. "I must see if Ebenezer's chair is still holding him and his laugh." And he told Granny about the stout chair, and they all had a hearty laugh.

"Father, do you suppose there will be any of the seeds of the biggest hollyhock still hanging on?" Tim asked anxiously.

"I could not say," his father answered absently, thinking of other things.

Night was falling as they went down the hills into Charlestown. When they reached the big Clive house, they knocked at the kitchen door, shut now against the cold sea breeze. Hannah opened the door. Pulling them inside, she clucked over them like an old hen over her chicks.

Tim went in search of Ebenezer. He found him in the stable rubbing down the sleek gray horses.

"Well, well! If it is not Tim, back from vaga-bonding. I must tell the Tinker that the chair he built is still as stout as ever." He leaned against the doorframe and laughed.

Tim laughed, too, to see his shaking stomach. But there was something that he must know at once. "Ebenezer, I lost the seeds of the biggest hollyhock. That is, I spilled them and the geese

[135]

gobbled them. You wouldn't have any saved, would you?" The boy peered at the gardener worriedly.

The gardener sobered. "Not any, lad. The garden is cleared and neat for the winter. And not a seed of the hollyhock did I save." But when Ebenezer began to scratch his head, Tim began to hope. For the big man could often scratch some very fine idea into his mind. "Tell you what, though, there are a few new plants we do not need. Come."

The gardener got a spiked tool. Tim followed him to the garden and stood watching him dig around a young hollyhock plant. Deeper and deeper he dug, until he could loosen the long center root. Then another, and another, he took from the soil. Three! Tim could hardly believe his eyes.

"Now, pay attention," Ebenezer ordered. "See, I will pack earth around the roots and wrap them in cloth. Do not unwrap them until you are ready to put them in the earth again. Be sure to dig the holes deep, so the earth can be packed around the

[136]

roots down their whole length." Tim watched and listened.

"Will they have blooms on them next summer?" Tim asked eagerly.

"Indeed, yes. The seed would have taken two years, and by then Dorcas would have been too much of a lady to play with dolls, like as not," said the gardener.

Tim trotted along to see Ebenezer put the plants in a corner of the cart. "You are a prince, Ebenezer!" Tim told him, with shining eyes.

Ebenezer guffawed. "A big prince I would make!"

Hannah and Granny were fast friends by the time they had all eaten supper in the cheery kitchen. Ebenezer squirmed in his stout chair, and laughed extra heartily, to show the Tinker how well he had done his work.

"Do you still have Granny's jar with the pewter lid, Tim?" Hannah asked.

"Granny has it now." Tim remembered how scared he had been in that kitchen, when Dame Clive had found him looking at it.

"And there will be no more witches to scare him into breaking this one." Granny was looking happier each day as they came nearer home, Tim thought.

The next day they set out on the last stretch of their homeward journey. Even the Hollyhock Lady came to stand with Hannah and Ebenezer, as they bid them good-by.

The crossing of the river near Medford hindered their haste, for a farmer must be talked into carrying the cart across the stream, piece by piece, in his boat. They spent a night at a farmhouse beyond Medford, where the Tinker mended for their fare. Another night they spent at The Anchor in Lynn. Tim must run to show their friend, the cobbler, how well his moccasins had served him in his vagabonding.

Lucy raised her head and whinnied knowingly as they came near Salem. Granny got off the cart and walked ahead, so she might catch the first glimpse of the town against the blue sea. Tears of joy ran down her cheeks. There it was, a little sea town on a sunny, November day.

When they came to the cottage, the Tinker unbarred the door and windows. The floor had been freshly scrubbed. Kindling and logs had been laid on the swept hearth, ready for coals to set it crackling.

Granny set out for the Whitcombs' to get live coals, Tim tagging along. Carefully he held his armload of the biggest hollyhock plants.

Dorcas came to open the door and as she saw them she gave a glad little screech. "Betsy! Betsy! See who has come!"

Betsy turned from the loom in the corner. "Granny Tetlow! Oh, Granny! And Tim! I knew you would be coming before long."

Granny smiled. "So I saw. It was you who scrubbed our floor, and laid our fire."

"It was little, for all you have done for us." Betsy brought little Hugh from his cradle to show to them. He gurgled at them happily. "He could be nothing but well, with all Daisy's good milk," she said, trying to make him show his new tooth.

"We have a cow of our own now. Her name is Star," Dorcas piped up proudly.

[139]

Tim stood first on one foot then the other, wishing that Dorcas would notice what he held in his arms. At last she came close to peep curiously at his burden.

"Hollyhocks — the biggest ones I ever saw. And they will have hollyhock dolls on them next summer," Tim said.

"Oh, Tim!" Dorcas breathed. "Then you are not angry at me now?" Tim shook his head emphatically. "Must they be put in the earth?"

"Do you think they will grow in the air?" Tim jested.

It was nice to see Dorcas dancing down the garden path ahead of him, his friend again. Tim worked hard, digging the holes deep and wide, as Ebenezer had said. Tim put the long, slim root down straight, and Dorcas held it so, as Tim packed the cold dirt around it. It was hard work, which took a long while, until the three plants were in the ground.

Dorcas's eyes sparkled as Tim told her about Dame Clive, the big house in Charlestown, and about Hannah and Ebenezer. He told her, too, of the work and jollity at Uncle Ezra's house in Worcester.

Dorcas clasped her hands. "There, it is finished. Tim, I would rather have these than all the queen's jewels!" And Tim felt quite pleased with himself.

He put his hand in his pocket and found there his favorite top, which Seth and Polly liked to spin with him, though John and Ethan would not. His hand closed on the pretty pebbles and shells that he and the boys of Salem had found and treasured. There were the willow whistles he had made on the way home; for what, he did not know then. Now he knew.

"I must go now," he murmured, backing away toward the path. Dorcas looked disappointed. "I'll be back sometime soon," he called, walking away quite fast.

At home, Granny had the fire roaring and had begun to mix dough in the wooden trough she used. "Granny, I'd like to see the wharves." He watched her deft fingers working in the yellow mass.

"Very well, but do not be gone long," she gave permission.

Tim went through the town past the church and townhouse, past the jail, where those accused of witchcraft were still held, though their sentences had been stayed. At last he reached the wharves.

Two boys were standing on the long dock, absorbed in something they held in their hands. When he went a little closer he could see plainly

[142]

that they were John and Ethan. Ethan held a small ship with white sails, while John labored to fasten a cord to its bow. Tim's heart beat like a mallet on wood, he was so filled with longing and anxiety. Then the two looked up and saw him.

"It is Tim!" Ethan shouted. He sounded glad.

"Come help us sail the boat!" John called.

Tim walked toward them, still doubtful of their good will. "Where did you get such a fine boat?" he asked, to see if they would answer him.

John grinned at him. "I whittled it out with the jackknife you threw away that morning we behaved so daft." He reached into his pocket and drew out Tim's knife. Then he pushed it into Tim's hand.

Tim held it unbelievingly, looking from John to Ethan. His throat felt tight. Why did your throat always feel that way when you were either glad or sad, he wondered.

Ethan tittered. "I laugh every time I remember how you pitched into John that day you left Salem."

John laughed, too, and Tim had to grin a little,

[143]

looking at them. "I — I lost my wits," Tim admitted.

"You would have whaled me right, if the Tinker had not pulled us apart," John chuckled. "And we had really gone there to take your knife to you."

"You — did?" Dismay followed surprise across Tim's reddening countenance.

Ethan dug John in the ribs, and they stood laughing at the look on Tim's face.

John gave the cord a final twist with his strong, blunt fingers, and took the boat from Ethan. "Come sail it," said the shipbuilder's son, and set off toward the end of the wharf.

Tim and Ethan followed more slowly. "I whittled out a doll for my sister with your knife — I hope you do not mind," Ethan said.

"Oh, no. The day you shouted that Granny was a witch and that I was bewitched, I was coming to offer you the loan of my knife." Tim stole a look at Ethan, then put an arm across his shoulders. Strange how mixed up we have all been, he thought to himself. Aloud he said, "Ethan, I want

you to show me how to make a doll. I'll whittle
one for Dorcas Whitcomb to play with until her
hollyhock dolls bloom next summer." Ethan
nodded his head. "And the loan of the knife is
yours and John's any time."

When Tim put the jackknife in his pocket he
found the forgotten whistles. He gave them to his
friends, telling how he had made them with his
father's knife.

John tried out his whistle. "Your father must
be a kind man to let you use his knife, after you
threw the knife away," he said wistfully.

"That he is," Tim said, pride shining from his
eyes.

Ethan admired his whistle from all sides. Then
he blew a loud blast.

Sailing the boat, and with all their talk, it was
soon time for Tim to go fetch Daisy from the
pasture. He scampered across town and nearly
ran into a big man as he came from his doorway.
The man caught Tim by the shoulder, whirling
him about.

"Where does thee think thee is bound for? And

with such haste!" The man stood looking down at Tim with twinkling eyes.

"Quaker Heath!" Tim gasped.

"Some day there will be room in the jail, and a red-headed lad I know may well land there, if thee does not keep in mind that the magistrates still frown upon haste and merriment."

Tim chuckled. "I'll try to remember," he promised.

That night, after Daisy had been milked and they had eaten, the Tetlow family sat around the crackling fire and talked of their homecoming. With glowing face Tim told of his meeting with John and Ethan.

There was a pleased look on his father's face, too. "Everywhere I went, folks stopped me to know when I would be coming to their house to mend."

Granny nodded her head. "Did I not say that the townspeople would come to their senses, and friends would be friends once more?"

"And wise you are, Mother," the Tinker smiled. "But, Tim, do remember that we have the tithing

[146]

men to look after our conduct, and that we must not offend the Church Fathers."

"Yes, Father." Tim gazed at the pictures that formed in the dancing flames. He could imagine that he heard Ebenezer's shaking laughter, Hannah's hearty voice, and all the merry sounds about Aunt Susie Williams's house. "Father, will we never be vagabonds again, now that Salem folks are friends?"

The Tinker pushed back a log in the great fireplace, sending clouds of sparks up the chimney. With a half smile he quirked an eyebrow at his son. "New friends and old friends, who can say which are best, eh, lad?" His father sat rubbing his hands together before the fire. "But now that you have your jackknife again, it might be well to begin making some new spokes for the cart wheels."

Tim winked at the flame pictures.